SHOOT TO KILL

The three punchers burst into the woods and one jerked his pistol up.

Fargo shot him. He aimed at the man's shoulder but the man shifted just as he squeezed the trigger and he was sure the slug hit lower. "Drop your hardware!" he bellowed at the other two.

Instead of obeying, one veered to the right and the other to the left. Fargo swung behind an oak. It wasn't much cover but he hoped it would cause them to break away and hunt cover of their own.

It didn't.

Yipping like Apaches, the two Texans closed on him, their six-guns blazing.

Slivers exploded from the oak and several stung Fargo's face. He aimed at the rider on the right, and fired. This time he didn't try for the shoulder; he shot dead-center and the man's arms flew back and his legs flew up and he tumbled over the back of his saddle.

THE
TRAILSMAN
#362

RANGE WAR
by
Jon Sharpe

A SIGNET BOOK

SIGNET
Published by New American Library, a division of
Penguin Group (USA) Inc., 375 Hudson Street,
New York, New York 10014, USA
Penguin Group (Canada), 90 Eglinton Avenue East, Suite 700, Toronto,
Ontario M4P 2Y3, Canada (a division of Pearson Penguin Canada Inc.)
Penguin Books Ltd., 80 Strand, London WC2R 0RL, England
Penguin Ireland, 25 St. Stephen's Green, Dublin 2,
Ireland (a division of Penguin Books Ltd.)
Penguin Group (Australia), 250 Camberwell Road, Camberwell, Victoria 3124,
Australia (a division of Pearson Australia Group Pty. Ltd.)
Penguin Books India Pvt. Ltd., 11 Community Centre, Panchsheel Park,
New Delhi - 110 017, India
Penguin Group (NZ), 67 Apollo Drive, Rosedale, Auckland 0632,
New Zealand (a division of Pearson New Zealand Ltd.)
Penguin Books (South Africa) (Pty.) Ltd., 24 Sturdee Avenue,
Rosebank, Johannesburg 2196, South Africa

Penguin Books Ltd., Registered Offices:
80 Strand, London WC2R 0RL, England

First published by Signet, an imprint of New American Library,
a division of Penguin Group (USA) Inc.

First Printing, December 2011
10 9 8 7 6 5 4 3 2 1

The first chapter of this book previously appeared in *Utah Deadly Double*, the three
hundred sixty-first volume in this series.

Copyright © Penguin Group (USA) Inc., 2011
All rights reserved

 REGISTERED TRADEMARK—MARCA REGISTRADA

The Trailsman

Beginnings . . . they bend the tree and they mark the man. Skye Fargo was born when he was eighteen. Terror was his midwife, vengeance his first cry. Killing spawned Skye Fargo, ruthless, cold-blooded murder. Out of the acrid smoke of gunpowder still hanging in the air, he rose, cried out a promise never forgotten.

The Trailsman they began to call him all across the West: searcher, scout, hunter, the man who could see where others only looked, his skills for hire but not his soul, the man who lived each day to the fullest, yet trailed each tomorrow. Skye Fargo, the Trailsman, the seeker who could take the wildness of a land and the wanting of a woman and make them his own.

*The Guadalupes, New Mexico, 1859—
where lonely summits loom over a
forbidding land of the lawless.*

1

Out of the dark mountains rose a howl that made the man by the campfire sit up and take notice. Loud and fierce, it was unlike any howl he'd ever heard. It echoed off the high peaks and was swept away by the wind into the black pitch of the night.

Broad of shoulder and narrow at the hips, Skye Fargo wore buckskins and a white hat turned brown with dust. A red bandanna, boots, and a well-used Colt at his hip completed his attire. He held his tin cup in both hands and glanced at his Ovaro. "What the hell was that?"

Fargo made his living as a scout, among other things. He'd wandered the west from Canada to Mexico and from the muddy Mississippi River to the broad Pacific Ocean. In his travels he'd heard hundreds of howling wolves and yipping coyotes and not a few wailing dogs, but he'd never, ever, heard anything like the cry that just startled him. More bray than howl, it was as savage and raw as the land around him.

Fargo settled back and sipped some coffee. Whatever it was, the thing was a ways off. He leaned on his saddle.

"In a week we'll be in Dallas. Oats and a warm stall for you and a fine filly and whiskey for me."

The Ovaro had raised its head and pricked its ears at the howl. Now it looked at him and lowered its head to go back to dozing.

"Some company you are," Fargo said, and chuckled. He drained the tin cup and set it down.

By the stars it was pushing midnight. Fargo intended to get a good rest and be up at the crack of dawn. He was deep in the Guadalupe Mountains, high on a stark ridge that overlooked the Hermanos Valley. A ring of boulders hid his fire from unfriendly eyes.

This was Apache country, and outlaws were as thick as fleas on an old hound.

Fargo laced his fingers on his chest and closed his eyes. He was on the cusp of slumber when a second howl brought him to his feet with his hand on his Colt.

This one was a lot closer.

The Ovaro raised its head again. It sniffed and stomped a hoof, a sure sign it had caught the animal's scent and didn't like the smell.

Fargo circled the fire to the stallion. He wasn't overly worried. Wolves rarely attacked people, and despite the strangeness of the howl, it had to be a wolf. He waited for a repeat of the cry and when more than five minutes went by and the night stayed quiet, he shrugged and returned to his blankets and the saddle.

"I'm getting jumpy," he said to the Ovaro.

Pulling his hat brim low, Fargo made himself comfortable. He thought about the lady waiting for him in Dallas and the fine time they would have. She was an old acquaintance with a body as young and ripe as a fresh strawberry, and she loved to frolic under the sheets as much as he did. He couldn't wait.

Sleep claimed him. Fargo dreamed of Mattie and that body of hers. They were fit to bust a four-poster bed when another howl shattered his dream. Instantly awake, he was out from under his blanket with the Colt in his hand before the howl died.

The short hairs at the nape of Fargo's neck pricked. The howl had been so near, he'd swear the thing was right on top of him.

The Ovaro was staring intently at a gap between two of the boulders.

Fargo sidled toward it. Warily, he peered out and broke into gooseflesh.

A pair of eyes glared back at him. Huge eyes, like a wolf's except that no wolf ever grew as large as the thing glaring at him. In the glow of the fire they blazed red like the eyes of a hell-spawned demon.

For all of ten seconds Fargo was riveted in disbelief. Then the red eyes blinked and the thing growled, and he shook himself and thumbed back the hammer. At the *click* the eyes vanished; they were there and they were gone, and he thought he heard the scrape of pads on rock.

Breathless, Fargo backed to the Ovaro. The thing might be after the stallion.

As the minutes crawled on claws of tension and silence reigned, he told himself the beast must be gone.

Fargo reclaimed his seat. He added fuel to the fire and refilled his battered tin cup. He'd wait a while before turning in.

From time to time Fargo had heard tales of wild animals bigger than most. Up in the geyser country there once roamed a grizzly the size of a log cabin, or so the old trappers liked to say. The Dakotas told a story about a white buffalo twice the size of any that ever breathed. Up Canada way, several tribes claimed that deep in the woods there lived hairy giants.

Fargo never gave much credence to the accounts. Tall tales were just that, whether related by white men or red men. He didn't believe in giants and goblins. But those eyes he saw weren't made by any ordinary-sized critter.

Fargo shrugged and put them from his mind. The thing had gone. The Ovaro was safe and he should get some sleep. He put down the cup and eased back on his saddle but it was a long while before he succumbed. The slightest noise woke him with a start.

Then came a noise that wasn't so slight—a scream torn from a human throat.

2

For the second time that night Fargo's skin crawled. He pushed to his feet and moved past the boulders.

The scream was borne to him out of the valley below. It keened to a high, ululating pitch, and ended as abruptly as the snuffing of a candle.

Fargo could tell the screamer was a man, possibly young, and were he to wager on it, probably dead. He probed the veil of darkness for sign of another fire or the light from a dwelling. There was none. Were he to go searching, he might stumble around until daybreak and not find the victim.

Suddenly, from the same vicinity as the scream, rose a piercing howl trilling with ferocity, the same as earlier.

The implication was obvious; whatever had paid him a visit had attacked someone else.

Fargo returned to the fire and pondered. By rights it was none of his affair. He could skirt the valley and push on to Dallas and a high time with his lady friend. He decided that was what he would do and after a while he turned in. Sleep proved elusive. He was lucky if he'd slept two full hours by the time pink splashed the eastern horizon. He chewed a piece of pemmican and finished the rest of the coffee and was in the saddle when the sun gave birth to the new day.

For a moment Fargo paused. Then, instead of reining aside to skirt the valley as he'd intended, he swore and tapped his spurs and rode down into it.

Hermanos Valley was eleven miles long and half that wide. Lush grass covered the valley floor, bordered by timber on the lower slopes. As Fargo recollected, it had been a haven for sheepherders since the days of Spanish rule.

The valley was unique in that above the timberline, a quarter-mile-wide bench, rich with grass, made for more excellent graze. As he neared it he saw hundreds of woolly white shapes.

In a clatter of rocks and pebbles the Ovaro came down the last slope and Fargo drew rein. The nearest sheep showed no alarm. Most ignored him.

Fargo clucked to the stallion. After a dozen yards the Ovaro whinnied and tossed its head and came to a stop of its own accord.

A splash of red in the green grass told Fargo why. Palming his Colt, he dismounted and advanced on foot.

The body was on its back, the face contorted in terror. The throat was a shredded cavity; it had literally been ripped out. A few flies were crawling in and around the ruin. Scarlet drops had spattered a serape and the white cotton shirt and pants.

It was a boy, not more than fifteen or sixteen, Fargo judged. Whatever attacked him had killed him swiftly. Other than a few claw marks, the clothes were untouched.

Fargo hunkered and cast about for sign. The grass was flattened in spots but there were no paw prints.

Fargo frowned and stood and shoved the Colt into his holster. He had no means to dig a grave other than his hands.

A broken limb from the timber below would suffice, and he went to the Ovaro and gripped the reins and was about to climb on when behind him a rifle lever ratcheted.

"Stand where you are, gringo, or I will kill you."

Fargo didn't know which surprised him more, that he had been taken unawares, or that the speaker was female. He looked over his shoulder and almost whistled in appreciation.

She was twenty or so, with flowing black hair, lustrous in the sun. Her beautiful dark eyes, at the moment smoldering with anger, were highlighted by long lashes. Her face was the kind that would cause men on the street to stop and stare. She wore a plain dress that covered her from her neck to her ankles but couldn't hide her charms.

"*Buenos días*," Fargo said, and smiled.

She put her cheek to her rifle and sighted on his chest. "Gringo pig."

"We're starting off on the wrong foot," Fargo said. "What did I do that you treat me like this?"

She nodded toward the body. "You killed Ramon, *bastardo*."

"I tore his throat out with my teeth?" Fargo said. "Be sensible."

"Where is it?" she asked.

"Where's what?"

"The dog you gringos use to kill us."

Fargo's patience was fraying. He didn't like staring into the muzzle of her rifle. Any moment her finger might twitch. "Lady, I don't know what in hell you're talking about."

"Sure you don't," she said, and wagged her weapon. "Unbuckle your gun belt and let it fall. I am taking you back. At last we have caught one of you, and we will do to you as you have done to us."

Fargo was confident he could dive to one side and draw and shoot her before she shot him but he had no desire to harm her.

"What's your name?"

"Delicia."

Fargo couldn't help it; he chuckled.

"What?"

"Nothing," Fargo said.

"Take off your gun belt, senor."

"I'll explain this to you just once. I had nothing to do with this. I'm on my way to Dallas. I heard a wolf last night . . ." Fargo paused. "At least, I think it was a wolf. And later I heard a scream that must have been Ramon. I just found his body, and that's all there is to it."

"I don't believe you," Delicia said.

"What reason would I have to lie?"

"You are one of them."

"One of who, damn it?"

"You know." Delicia put her cheek to the rifle again. "I will not say it again, senor. Unbuckle your *pistola* or I will shoot you." Her jaw tightened and her eyes grew hard with determination.

Fargo had no doubt she would. He could kill her, or he could go along for the time being. Slowly lowering his right hand, he pried at his belt buckle. "You're making a mistake."

"No, gringo," Delicia said. "You are the one who has made a mistake, and before this day is over, you will pay for it with your miserable life."

3

At the north end of the valley was a spring. Ten wagons, varying in length from twelve to sixteen feet, were parked in a half circle around it. The sides and the backs were wood, the tops were canvas curved tight over hoops. The back wheels were slightly larger than the front, and the tongues lay on the ground.

The teams were in a string near the spring.

Fargo had seen similar wagons before. Sheepherders throughout the West used them. From the number, he gathered that more than one family shared the graze in the Hermanos Valley.

Fargo slowly approached, leading the Ovaro with the body of Ramon over the saddle, Delicia trailing after him with her rifle pointed at his back.

Beyond the crescent of wagons, the sheepherders were going about their daily routines. Most were simply dressed in the cotton clothes they favored. Some of the women had colorful shawls and belts. Some of men wore serapes and ponchos. White hats were much in evidence, although a few wore black.

There looked to be thirty females or more, running in age from about seventy down to small children, and about the same number of men. Several campfires were crackling, and the aroma of food and coffee was tantalizing.

Fargo went around a wagon tongue into the camp.

At a yell from a youth, the sheepherders stopped what they were doing and converged. A considerable commotion ensued. Ramon was examined amid gasps of dismay. A middle-aged woman burst into tears. Voices were raised in anger, and two brawny men turned on Fargo and seized him by the arms and a third man drew a knife from under a poncho and advanced with it held low to thrust.

"Now wait a minute," Fargo said.

"*Te matare*, gringo," the man with the knife said.

"*Parar!*" a voice shouted, and from out of the throng came an old man. Slightly stooped from age, he nonetheless had a powerful build and a commanding presence. He wore a red cap and sported a bushy mustache as white as his hair. The others parted to make way. He came to the Ovaro and gripped Ramon's hair and raised the head to see the wound. Sorrow etched his seamed features when he faced Fargo. "*Habla usted español?*"

"*Si*," Fargo answered. "But I'm better at English."

"English it will be, then," the old man said with no trace of an accent. "I am Porfiro, the leader here."

"Skye Fargo."

Porfiro motioned at Ramon. "Did you have anything to do with this?"

"No."

"He lies," Delicia said angrily.

"You have proof he lies?" Porfiro asked.

"I went up to take food to Ramon," Delicia said. "Instead I found his body, as you see it. Then I heard a horse coming down the mountain. I hid, and this man came out of the trees and went to the body."

"That is your proof?"

"He is one of them, I tell you," Delicia declared, her rifle still trained on Fargo.

"One of who?" Fargo said.

Porfiro appraised him from hat to boots. "I think not," he said. "Look at how he dresses."

"*Excusa?*" Delicia said.

Raising his voice, Porfiro said in Spanish, "Look at him, all of you. Look at what he wears. Buckskins. These are the clothes of a hunter or a scout. They are not the clothes of our enemies."

"You can not judge by that," the man with the knife said.

Porfiro turned to Fargo. "Do you understand what I told them? Am I right?"

"I've done a lot of scouting for the army," Fargo said. He worked at other jobs, too, from time to time, but a scout described him as well as anything.

9

"See?" Porfiro addressed the others.

"And you are willing to take his word?" demanded a woman almost as old as he was.

"If he is one of them, he would lie to save himself," a man in a poncho said.

"One of who?" Fargo again asked.

It was the old woman who answered him. "The invaders." She gazed off down the Hermanos Valley. "For hundreds of years our people have grazed our sheep here, from when these mountains and this valley were part of the Imperial Spanish Viceroyalty of New Spain. We graze them and shear them and take our wool to market, and we are happy and content." Her gaze became a glare. "But now *they* have come. From the south, from Texas. With their cows and their guns. And they say that they are going to graze their cattle and we must leave." She raised a gnarled fist and shook it. "Us! Leave! When my father and mother grazed their sheep here, and their father and mother before them, and theirs before them."

Her outburst caused a ripple of muttering and hard looks cast at Fargo.

"I don't care what Porfiro says," said the man with the knife. "We should kill this one and send him back to his friends as a warning." And with that, he reached for Fargo's throat.

4

Porfiro swatted the knife aside, stepped between them, and folded his arms across his chest. "To hurt him you must first hurt me. Are you willing to do that, my grandson?"

"Carlos, no!" the old woman exclaimed.

Two other men, advanced in years but robust and vigorous, moved protectively to either side of Porfiro, and the one on the right said, "Listen to your grandmother, boy."

"Porfiro is our leader," said the other. "Harm him and you will be an outcast."

Carlos glanced from one to the other and then at his grandmother. "You old ones always stick together, eh?"

"We have our laws, boy, and they will be obeyed," said the man on the right.

"Quit calling me that," Carlos snapped. He took a step back and held his hands up, palms out. "And I would never hurt my grandfather, were he our *líder* or not. I am of his blood, and blood is always to be honored."

The sheepherder in the poncho impatiently waved a hand. "All this petty bickering is bad enough, but we still have to decide what to do with this Buckskin."

"My name is Fargo," Fargo said.

"I will have a talk with him," Porfiro said, and gestured at the men who had hold of Fargo's arms. They reluctantly let go.

"I'm obliged," Fargo said.

"Ven conmigo," Porfiro replied, and ushered him to the rear of a wagon. Opening a small door, he motioned for Fargo to precede him.

Fargo had never been in a sheepherder's wagon before. He'd figured there would be seats, like in a stagecoach, or maybe it would be littered with personal effects, like in a Conestoga. But it was nothing like either.

The wagon was a home on wheels. There was a small stove. There were cupboards and shelves. There was a table. There was even a bed big enough for two, with a flowered quilt. Along one side was a bench, built as part of the wall. The interior smelled of pipe smoke and food.

"My humble home," Porfiro said. He indicated the bench.

Fargo sat and placed his hands on his knees. "The girl took my Colt," he mentioned. "I'd like it back."

"First things first." Porfiro sank down and thoughtfully studied him. "Were you telling the truth about not harming Ramon?"

"Like I told Delicia, what reason would I have?" Fargo countered.

"Our enemies don't need a reason other than we tend sheep and they tend cattle," Porfiro said. "Ramon is not the first one of us to have his throat torn out by their dog. He is the third."

"It wasn't a dog," Fargo said.

Porfiro sat up. "You have seen it?"

"I saw its eyes," Fargo said.

"We have heard it howl at night, as a dog does."

Fargo was going to point out that wolves howled, too. Instead he said, "And you say the cowboys are using this dog to try and drive your people off?"

"*Si*, senor," Porfiro said. "Until they came our valley was peaceful."

"Where are these cowboys? I didn't see any sign of them."

"At the south end of the valley," Porfiro revealed. "There are eight of them and they brought over a hundred cows."

"That's all?"

"I know what you are thinking. But they have many guns and we have only a few. And besides, I do not believe in killing." Porfiro sadly bowed his head. "A lot more of them are coming, senor, along with a great many more cattle."

"They told you this?"

"*Si*. When they first came, they invited us to eat with them and some of us went. We thought they were passing through, as you gringos say. But that was not the case. They told us they are making Hermanos Valley part of their range, and we must take our sheep and leave. Can you imagine?"

Yes, Fargo could. Cattlemen and sheepmen were always at odds. In Texas and elsewhere they had clashed and spilled blood on both sides. With more and more cattle ranches starting up thanks to the demand for beef from back East, the problem was bound to get worse. "I'm sorry for your troubles."

Porfiro looked at him. "I almost believe you mean it."

"I do," Fargo said. He was a firm believer in every man, and woman, being allowed to live as they damn well pleased without interference from anybody.

Porfiro's brow knit and he bit his lower lip. "You sound sincere, senor. I wonder . . ."

"Wonder what?" Fargo prompted when he didn't go on.

"I wonder if you would be willing to help us."

"Help you how?"

"Go to these cowboys. Talk to them on our behalf. Plead with them to take their cows and go before more lives are lost."

"I doubt they'd listen."

"You are a gringo, as they are."

Fargo laughed. "That doesn't count for much. If I was one of them, if I was a cowboy, it might. But to them I'm as much an outsider as you are." He shook his head. "It wouldn't do any good."

Just then there was a knock on the door and in came Delicia. She stopped and put her hands on her hips and glared at Fargo.

"What do you want, granddaughter?" Porfiro asked.

"Granddaughter?" Fargo said.

"We are all of us related in one manner or another," Porfiro said.

Delicia tapped a foot. "I want to know what he has been telling you. You are too trusting, grandfather. We should have done as Carlos wanted and slit his throat."

"I love you, too," Fargo said, and winked.

A red flush spread from Delicia's neckline to her hairline. "You are not nearly as funny as you think you are."

"For your information," Porfiro said, "I have asked him to go to the cowboys on our behalf and ask them to leave our valley."

"You did what?"

"He declined."

"Of course he did," Delicia said. "What does he care if we live or die? He is no better than they are. If we were not in your wagon I would spit on him."

"There are better ways of swapping spit," Fargo said.

Delicia balled her small fists. "I think I am beginning to hate you."

"I want to make love to you, too," Fargo said.

She took a step and hissed through clenched teeth. "You are the most aggravating man I have ever met."

Fargo winked again. "That's why you want me."

Porfiro snorted.

"Don't encourage him," Delicia said. "He is playing with us. He doesn't know how to be serious."

"Tell you what," Fargo said, grinning. "I'll go talk to them for ten kisses."

"What?"

"I'll talk to these cowboys and after I get back you give me ten kisses."

"*Estas loco*, gringo," Delicia said. "You're crazy. I will do no such thing."

"Afraid you'd like it too much?"

She became even redder. "Grandfather, how can you sit there and let him talk to me like this?"

"You are a grown woman. Fight your own fights," Porfiro said.

Fargo stood. "That's all right. I figured she wouldn't go for it. She must not care for her people as much as she claims."

"How dare you?" Delicia said, and poised to throw herself at him. But she must have changed her mind because she straightened and said, "Very well. Go talk to them for us. And when you get back, you shall have your ten kisses."

"Better practice your puckering," Fargo said.

5

Hermanos Valley wound like a snake. Here and there fingers of forest and rocky spines thrust from either side so that at most only a quarter-mile stretch was visible at any one time.

Fargo rode at a walk. The day was bright and warm. For the first few miles he'd passed hundreds of sheep. After that there was only grass until he came on a few cattle and after that a few more. He was surprised not to find any cowboys.

Porfiro had been right; their camp was at the south end of the valley. Eight of them were sitting around a fire drinking coffee and talking and laughing. They didn't spot him until he was well around the last bend. Jumping up, they came to meet him, some with their hands on their six-shooters.

"Hell, he ain't one of them," the youngest cowboy declared. "They don't wear buckskins, and he ain't Spanish."

A tall man in chaps with a scar on his left cheek took a few steps in front of the rest. High on his right hip was a Remington. "Howdy, mister. We took you for a sheepherder and almost shot you."

Fargo drew rein and leaned on the saddle horn. "Nurse-maiding a bunch of woollies isn't for me." He didn't add that neither was nursemaiding cows. Not that he had anything against either profession. He liked to wander too much—to always see what was over the horizon—to ever settle into a steady job.

"What do you do?"

"Scout, mostly," Fargo said, and gave his name.

"Griff Wexler," the tall cowboy said in his pronounced Texas drawl. "I'm ramrod for the Bar T. Ever hear of it?"

Fargo vaguely recollected that it was one of the biggest outfits in west Texas. "You gents are a bit off your range," he remarked.

"Last fall a couple of the boys came up into the Guadalupes to hunt elk and stumbled on this here valley," Griff said. "When they got back they told Mr. Trask. He's always on the lookout for new graze."

"I saw a few cows," Fargo said.

"Before long there'll be thousands." Griff motioned at the fire. "Light and set a spell. We have coffee if you're of a mind."

"I'll take you up on that." Fargo dismounted. A couple of the cowboys nodded at him by way of greeting. A short puncher with a lot of muscle handed him a tin cup.

"Here you go, mister. Shorty is my handle."

Fargo hunkered and held the cup in both hands and sipped. "One thing about cowhands," he said by way of praise, "your coffee could float a horseshoe."

The youngest cowboy chuckled. "We use it to remove paint, too."

Griff Wexler had his thumbs hooked in his belt and was tapping the buckle. "So you saw the mangy sheep," he said.

"And the sheepherders."

A cowboy swore and spat and another patted his six-gun and said, "I'd like to put windows in their noggins."

"Did you talk to them?" Griff asked.

"They didn't give me much choice," Fargo said. "They thought I was one of you and hankered to slit my throat."

Griff looked at the others. "See? That proves what those mutton eaters think of us."

"Seems they blame you for killing three of their own," Fargo mentioned, and gazed about the camp. "But I don't see a dog anywhere."

At his comment all the cowboys stiffened and Griff Wexler said, "What's that about a dog?"

"They claim you set one loose on them."

"That's a damned lie," Griff declared. "They said that to make us look bad."

"I saw one of the herders with my own eyes," Fargo said. "His throat was torn out." He swallowed more coffee. "I saw the dog, too."

Griff took a step toward him. "You sure enough did?"

"I saw . . . something," Fargo said. "Its eyes, anyway. It came close to my fire last night."

16

"And it's killed three of those sheep lovers, you say?" another cowboy asked.

"So they told me."

"It don't make sense," Shorty said.

"No, it doesn't," Griff said. "Killin' them *and* our cows? What the hell is goin' on?"

"What was that about your cows?" Fargo said.

"Somethin' has been at them," Griff answered. "We found six so far clawed and bit to ribbons."

"But whatever killed them didn't eat any of the meat," another puncher remarked.

Fargo was as puzzled as they were. "It hasn't gone after any of you?"

Griff Wexler scowled. "Our third night here, we heard it howlin' off in the trees. Two nights later Shorty, there, was ridin' herd and . . ." He stopped. "Why don't you tell it, Shorty?"

"Not much to tell," Shorty said. "I was singin' to the cows to keep 'em calm and almost didn't hear the damn thing come up behind me. If my horse hadn't caught its scent and made a fuss, it would have jumped me. I'm sure of it." He stopped. "As it was, I turned and saw somethin' big slinkin' toward me. I drew my pistol and shot at it but I was so spooked I missed and the thing ran off."

"What was it?"

"Beats the hell out of me," Shorty replied. "All I know is it's big and has a long tail."

"That leaves out a bear," another cowhand said. "Bears ain't got tails to speak of."

Griff was scratching his head. "I reckoned maybe the sheepherders sent it after us but now you say it's after them, too. What in hell is goin' on?"

"If I can find its tracks I can tell you what it is," Fargo said. He had more experience at tracking than most any man alive.

"Good luck, mister," Griff said. "Those cows that were killed? We looked all around their bodies and there wasn't a print of the thing anywhere."

"There had to be."

"Did you find any around that dead sheepherder?"

Fargo shook his head.

"There you go," Griff said.

Fargo knew it was pointless but he had promised he would try so he said, "The sheepherders wanted me to give you a message."

"Did they, now?"

"They would be pleased as could be if you would kindly leave their valley."

Several cowboys cursed and muttered.

"*Their* valley?" Shorty angrily declared. "They never filed a claim on it. Our boss checked."

"How about you give them a message for us?" Griff said. "I'd go myself but they're liable to take a potshot at me before I can have my say."

"I suppose I could."

"Good." Griff's smile was vicious. "You tell those miserable mutton lickers that when the rest of our outfit gets here, we're goin' to run them and their hoofed locusts out. They'd best light a shuck while they can."

"What if they won't go?"

"That's fine with us," Griff said, and patted his Remington. "Whether they do or they don't, we'll be shed of them one way or the other."

"Damn right we will," Shorty said. "They don't leave, this valley will run red with blood."

6

It was late afternoon when Fargo started for the sheepherder camp. The sun was low on the horizon and the shadows in the timber had lengthened.

The Bar T hands had been friendly enough. He hadn't learned a whole lot, although one thing was certain: barring a miracle, Shorty's prediction was bound to come true.

Fargo took to thinking about Delicia and the ten kisses he'd earned. He grinned in anticipation—and suddenly became aware of movement on the slope above. He was close to the west edge of the valley, only a few yards from the tree line, and he saw . . . something . . . dart from behind a pine tree and around a thicket.

Drawing rein, Fargo palmed the Colt. He'd had only a glimpse but he was sure it wasn't a deer or an elk. It was too low to the ground. "I wonder," he said, and reined into the trees. There was a chance it might be the creature that killed Ramon and the others. Cocking his Colt, he warily approached the thicket.

The Ovaro didn't shy or whinny. He found out why when he rounded the thicket and a coyote lit off up the mountain. He didn't shoot it. Coyotes were seldom a threat. Not long ago he'd been tied to a tree by an enemy and several coyotes had tried to eat him but that was a special circumstance.

Fargo twirled the Colt into his holster and resumed his ride. The sun was halfway gone. It didn't worry him that the wolf or dog or whatever it was might soon be abroad. Shorty's experience suggested it was gun-shy.

If he had any sense, Fargo told himself, he'd be on his way to Dallas. He had no stake in the sheepmen/cattlemen war shaping up. He should make himself scarce and let them do as they will.

But there was Delicia.

Fargo envisioned her eyes and those long legs of hers and felt a twitch below his belt. He'd be the first to admit that women were his weakness. He liked bedding them more than he liked just about anything. Give him a willing filly, and a bottle or three of whiskey, and he was as content as a man could be.

Fargo smacked his lips. He wouldn't mind a drink right about now.

In the forest above, a twig snapped.

Once again Fargo brought the stallion to a halt. He scanned the woods but saw nothing. He was about to raise the reins when an uneasy feeling came over him, a feeling he sometimes had when unseen eyes were watching. He sat and waited but except for a pair of sparrows flitting gaily about, the woodland was still.

As a precaution Fargo reined away from the tree line until he was a hundred yards out. Then he continued to the north. His unease persisted. It could be that whatever was up in the trees was shadowing him. Then again, how did he know it was a *what* and not a *who*? He wondered if one of the cowboys was keeping an eye on him.

Before long, the sun sank. The blue sky changed to gray and then black, and a sparkling legion of stars blossomed.

The fires and the lights in the sheepherder camp came into view.

Fargo thought again of Delicia, of the two of them alone in a wagon, of him pressing her warm body to his and—

The Ovaro whinnied.

Fargo swore. It was damned careless to let his attention lapse. He looked around but saw no cause for the stallion's agitation.

Smoke was curling from the stovepipes in the wagons. Others were doing their cooking over the campfires. Large pots hung on tripods and women were stirring the concoctions.

A boy spotted Fargo and yelled.

Once again the sheepherders converged. This time Porfiro was one of the first to reach him and when he raised an arm, the rest stopped.

"You came back. I thought we might have seen the last of you."

Fargo glanced at Delicia, who blushed. "I gave my word. I relayed your message."

"What did the cowboys say?"

Fargo gave it to them straight. "As soon as more of them show up they're driving you out."

Heated outbursts resulted. Curses were heaped on the punchers.

"Let them try!" Carlos cried. "They have more guns but we have right on our side."

"Big help that will be," Fargo said.

Delicia put her hands on her hips. "You mock our will to fight for what is ours?"

"You can't fight bullets with good intentions," Fargo said. "The bullets win every time."

"Did they say when they will come for us?" Porfiro asked.

"They don't have a set date," Fargo said. "It depends on when their big augur shows up."

"Their what?" a man asked.

"Ben Trask, the rancher they work for." Fargo alighted and grinned at Delicia. "Miss me?"

"Not even a little bit." She whirled and stalked off, her dress swirling about her long legs.

"That granddaughter of mine has fire in her veins," Porfiro said, smiling.

"She's isn't the only one," Carlos declared. He came past Porfiro and poked Fargo in the chest. "Stay away from my sister, gringo, if you know what is good for you."

"And if I don't?" Fargo said.

Carlos placed his hand on the hilt of his knife. "Three guesses," he said.

7

Porfiro let Fargo add the Ovaro to the string. Fargo stripped his saddle and saddle blanket and bridle off and slid them under Porfiro's wagon. The bottom was a good three feet off the ground so there was plenty of room.

By the time he strolled back to the fires and the cooking pots, the sheepherders were eating and drinking. Despite the news he'd brought, they were in good spirits. There was a lot of good-natured joking and laughing. They were close-knit, these people, and he admired them for that.

He heard his name called.

Porfiro was seated near a pot on a tripod. The old woman from earlier was stirring the contents with a large wooden spoon. She scowled as Fargo came over.

"I don't believe I have introduced you," Porfiro said. "This is the love of my life, Constanza."

"How do you do, ma'am," Fargo said.

"I was perfectly fine until the cowboys came," Constanza said. "Why can't your kind leave us alone?"

"Don't start," Porfiro said.

Constanza wagged the dripping spoon at him. "Don't tell me what to do. This man knows how much our valley means to me."

Fargo accepted a cup of coffee from Porfiro. "I can't speak for all whites, ma'am. Can you speak for all sheepherders?"

"All those here I can, yes," Constanza said. She resumed her stirring. "I am afraid, Senor Fargo. I fear for my people. Your gringos are too quick to anger and too quick to pull the trigger."

Fargo squatted and drank; the coffee had a chicory taste. "It's too bad there's not any law handy." The nearest town was hundreds of miles away. As for the army, patrols never came this far.

"We would not go to them in any event," Porfiro said with a suggestion of pride. "We handle our own difficulties."

"Between the *perro galgo* terrible and the Texas vaqueros, our lives are filled with strife," Constanza said sorrowfully.

"Is that what your people call that thing? The Terrible Hound?"

"Or just the Hound." Constanza looked at him. "You didn't see it at the cowboy camp?"

"They don't have a dog," Fargo said. "Whatever that thing is, it's been killing their cattle and tried to jump one of them. They thought it was your doing until I told them about the three of you it's killed."

"They lied," Constanza said. "It has to be theirs."

Porfiro stirred. "Can we talk about something else for once? I would like to relax and enjoy myself."

"Have you so soon forgotten Ramon? And the others?" Constanza chided.

"You know better, woman." Porfiro refilled his cup. To Fargo he said, "She is bitter, my wife. And I can't blame her."

"Ramon. Pedro. And poor sweet Angelita. She was only ten years old, and a joy to all." A tear trickled down Constanza's wrinkled cheek.

"Wait," Fargo said. "That hound or whatever the hell it is killed a little girl?"

"Angelita was the first," Porfiro said, his expression now as sad as his wife's. "A beautiful child. She always smiled. She was always so full of life."

"*Si*," Constanza softly echoed. "And now she is gone, killed by the beast those vaqueros deny having."

"It was the night after Angelita was slain that we first heard the howls," Porfiro mentioned. "They have chilled my blood ever since."

Fargo thought of Dallas, and the dove who was waiting, and sighed. "I have a proposition for you."

"Senor?"

"I'll hunt this thing down and kill it. It might take me a while but I'm a damn good tracker, if I say so myself."

"You would do this for us?"

Constanza turned from her pot. "Why?" she asked suspiciously.

"Do I have to have a reason?"

"What do you want in return?"

"Yes," said a voice behind Fargo, and Delicia came around and regarded him with the same suspicion. "What *do* you want in return?"

Fargo grinned. "A good start would be those ten kisses you owe me."

"I'm serious," Delicia said.

"So am I."

"We can pay you," Porfiro offered. "We aren't rich but between all of us I think I can collect almost a hundred dollars. Would that be enough?"

"Did I ask for money?"

"No one does something for nothing," Constanza said. "And a gringo, most especially, would not do a kindness for us out of the goodness of his heart. So I ask you again, senor. Why do you do this?"

"I don't much like the notion of little girls having their throats ripped out."

"That is all there is to it?"

"Constanza!" Porfiro exclaimed.

"That is all there is to it," Fargo said. But he was staring at Delicia.

8

After their evening meal the shepherds sat around their fires talking and relaxing. A small group had joined Porfiro, Constanza, Delicia and Carlos around theirs.

For a while no one paid much attention to Fargo, or if they looked his way, it was with open distrust. But when Porfiro mentioned that Fargo had offered to hunt the Terrible Hound, as they called it, they began to warm to him.

The turning point came when a small girl in a plain dress came over after Porfiro's announcement and stood in front of him with her small hands folded. "*Es cerito*, Senor Fargo?"

"*Si*," Fargo confirmed.

"I would like that. Angelita was my very best friend."

"Yoana, here, and Angelita were born only weeks apart," Porfiro said. "They grew up together and were rarely apart."

"You will kill the Hound, senor?" Yoana asked.

"I'll try my damnedest."

"Senor," Constanza scolded.

"Kill it," Yoana said in grim earnest, and placed a hand on Fargo's knee. "Kill it for Angelita and kill it for me."

"I'll try," Fargo said again.

"My *madre* and *padre* will not let me tend the sheep until it is dead. They are afraid it will do to me as it did to poor Angelita."

"You can't blame them."

"I miss the sheep," Yoana said. "I miss sitting in the sun and watching over them. I miss it very much."

Fargo drank some coffee.

"I am afraid, senor," Yoana went on. "I am afraid of the Hound and I am afraid of the vaqueros. Life was good before they came. I was happy." She lowered her arm. "If you kill the Hound I will be happy again."

"What about the cowboys?" Fargo asked. "Do you want them dead, too?"

"Oh, no, senor. They are people, like us. I wish they would go but I do not wish them dead."

Several adults nodded in agreement.

"I'll do what I can for all of you," Fargo heard himself saying.

From then on he was accepted. Not fully by some, though. Carlos and a few others were constantly casting looks that could kill.

About ten o'clock the little ones were trundled off to their wagons for bed. A lot of the mothers stayed with them so that it was mostly men and a few females left around the campfires.

Someone else had been casting looks at Fargo all night: Delicia. Her looks weren't laced with hate. They were looks Fargo had seen before, and they secretly made him smile.

About eleven, five sheepherders came out of the dark on horseback and five others climbed on and went out to replace them on night watch. All five were armed, three with old rifles and two with old Colt Dragoon revolvers. That was the extent of the sheepherders' armory.

"Normally we would not take guns or use horses," Porfiro mentioned. "But with the Hound . . ." He stopped and gestured.

Not a minute later the valley pealed to a bray so fierce that it prickled the short hairs at the nape of Fargo's neck.

"El perro terrible," a woman said, and crossed herself.

Fargo stood. "Reckon I'll go for a little ride," he announced.

Porfiro rose, too, and said, "It would be pointless for you to go after it now."

"I might get lucky," Fargo said. Truth was, all that coffee had him wide awake. An hour or two in the saddle and he'd be ready to turn in.

"Hermanos Valley is big, senor," Porfiro said. "For you to be lucky, as you say, would be like—" He paused. "What is that expression? Ah, yes. Like finding a needle in a haystack."

"It's worth trying." Fargo went to Porfiro's wagon, reclaimed his saddle blanket from underneath, and was smoothing it on the Ovaro when footsteps came up behind him.

"I wish you would rethink this, senor," Delicia said softly.

Fargo inhaled her musky scent as he turned. "I didn't know you cared."

Delicia averted her gaze. "I don't. I just don't want you dead on our account."

"Don't take up poker," Fargo said.

"Senor?"

"You don't lie well. Your face gives you away."

Her lips compressed and her eyes flashed. "I have no idea what you are talking about."

"Sure you don't," Fargo said, and kissed her on the mouth, a light, fleeting brush of his lips across hers.

Delicia didn't start or slap him. As calm as could be, she asked, "And what was that for?"

"The first of the ten you promised. Nine more to go." Fargo leaned toward her but she placed her hand on his chest.

"I get to choose when and where."

Fargo gestured at the well of ink around them. "What's wrong with here and now?"

"Someone might see."

"There's no one else around." Fargo grinned. "Admit it. You're scared."

"Of you, senor?" Delicia said, and uttered a forced laughed. "Why would I be scared of you?"

"Because you're afraid you might like it."

"You flatter yourself."

Delicia wheeled to go but Fargo took her by the shoulders, spun her around, and kissed her again, harder this time, his mouth lingering. Once again she didn't resist. But neither did she respond. When he pulled back, she smiled smugly.

"Was that what you call a kiss, senor? I would call it a brotherly peck."

"Would you, now?" Fargo said, and molded his body to hers.

He kissed her with ardor, his right hand roaming down her back to cup her bottom and his left cupping her breast.

Her body yielded and her tongue brushed his mouth. He was about to cup her other breast when the night was rent by a savage howl that seemed to come from only a few yards away—and a child screamed.

9

Delicia pushed away, exclaiming in horror, "The Hound is in our camp!"

Not in it but close by, as Fargo learned when he slicked his Colt, grabbed her wrist, and ran around the wagon. Everyone had leaped to their feet and the men were brandishing knives. Mothers poked their heads out of wagons to fearfully ask if the beast had slain another of them.

A ferocious bray focused all eyes on a patch of blackness to the west.

Fargo found himself standing near Porfiro.

"The Hound is close, senor. The closest it has ever come."

"And all our guns are with the men watching our sheep," someone lamented.

"I'm still here," Fargo said.

"Do something," a woman urged, "before it attacks and some of us die."

Fargo doubted that any carnivore short of a grizzly would dare come closer to so many campfires. He ran to the Ovaro and saddled it anyway. It took a bit, and when he returned, Porfiro and a knot of men were at the edge of the circle of light.

As Fargo drew rein the old man said, "We heard it growl, there." And he pointed.

"Build up the fires," Fargo suggested, "and don't let anyone stray off."

"No one would be that foolish, senor," Porfiro said.

Delicia ran up clutching a burning brand. "Here." She held it up. "You will need something to see by."

Fargo thanked her. Holding it aloft, he rode at a walk into the maw of night. A tiny voice railed at him for putting himself in peril. He didn't owe these people anything. He should light a shuck. Instead, he rode on, moving the torch back and forth.

The Ovaro nickered at the same instant that Fargo spied a pair of gleaming eyes. Big eyes, like those the night before.

He drew rein and raised the Colt.

The eyes disappeared.

"Not this time," Fargo said, and used his spurs. The glow of the torch washed over a long shape flowing low to the ground away from him. He rode faster, the flames flickering and dancing.

The Hound, if that is what it was, went faster, too.

It was making for the timber, Fargo realized, and if it reached the trees it stood a good chance of getting away. He was so intent on overtaking it that he didn't give much attention to the torch.

Suddenly a gust of wind caused it to sputter and nearly go out.

Fargo swore and slowed.

The shape pulled ahead and was soon lost in the pitch.

In frustration Fargo fired two swift shots. He doubted he hit it. He kept riding in the hope that the thing would circle back and try to jump him.

He had covered a quarter of a mile when hooves thudded and a pair of riders swept out of the west.

Fargo recognized them as two of the sheepherders who had ridden off earlier. Both were young and had mustaches. One carried a Sharps rifle, the other a Colt Dragoon.

"Senor Fargo!" the man with the Colt exclaimed. "Alejandro and I saw your torch and heard your shots."

"Did you kill the beast?" Alejandro eagerly asked. "Tell me it is dead."

Fargo shook his head.

The young man with the Colt cursed colorfully and shook the Colt at the empty air.

"Calm yourself, Flavio," Alejandro said. "At least he had a shot at it. That is more than any of us have been able to do."

"It is a demon," Flavio declared. "That is why no one can kill it."

"It's a dog or a wolf," Fargo said. "Nothing more."

"Did you see what it did to Ramon's throat, senor?" Flavio asked.

"I found Ramon, remember?"

"Show me a dog that can rip a man's throat out with one bite," Flavio said. "I say to you it is more than a dog, but what is the mystery."

Fargo had seen victims of dog attacks, and Flavio was wrong. Some dogs *could* rip out a throat—and do a lot worse.

A thought struck him. "Tell me something. How were the rest killed? Angelita and the other one?"

"By the Hound, senor," Flavio said, his tone suggesting the question was silly.

"No, he wants to know *how*," Alejandro said. "Both had their throats torn out, senor, as Ramon did."

"Do tell," Fargo said.

"Is that important?" Alejandro asked.

It had been Fargo's experience that dogs didn't always go for the throat. Some went for the arms or the legs or the body. "It could be."

"How so?"

"It's too soon to say yet," Fargo hedged. All he had at the moment were vague possibilities.

Flavio jabbed the Dragoon at the forested slope. "We should go after it while it is still near."

"We won't catch it," Alejandro said.

"We should *try*," Flavio argued. "We owe it to our people." He slapped his legs against his sorrel.

"We should go with him, senor," Alejandro urged, "to keep him from harm."

"I've got nothing better to do," Fargo said, but he was thinking of Delicia.

The torch lasted until they were almost to the trees.

Casting it down, Fargo drew rein. So did Alejandro. They could hear Flavio crashing about higher up, making a god-awful amount of racket.

"What is he doing, senor?"

"Scaring off every animal within ten miles," Fargo said.

Alejandro shouted his friend's name but Flavio didn't answer. "He is always so *impetuoso*." Alejandro jabbed his heels.

Fargo sighed and followed. He'd be surprised if the Hound was still in the vicinity.

Higher up, Flavio yelled something.

"Did you hear what he said, senor?" Alejandro asked. "I didn't catch it."

Neither did Fargo.

Then came another yell, louder and clearer: "The beast! I have found it! Hurry, Alejandro! Hurry!"

The boom of Flavio's Colt rolled down the slope and off across the valley.

"Flavio!" Alejandro cried.

Fargo brought the Ovaro to a gallop and swept past Alejandro. A second shot came from off to the left somewhere. Fargo veered in that direction.

There was a third shot, and a heartbeat later a strident whinny.

Flavio let out a shriek.

Behind Fargo, Alejandro was practically beside himself, screaming his friend's name.

Fargo caught movement. He burst into a clearing and beheld Flavio's horse on its side, struggling to rise. He also spotted Flavio on his belly with his arms flung out in appeal.

"Help me, senor!"

Something had hold of Flavio's leg and was pulling him into the undergrowth.

10

Flavio screamed and dug his fingers into the ground, trying to stop himself from being dragged off. But the creature that had hold of him was too powerful. "Help me!" he cried again.

Fargo resorted to his spurs and the Ovaro swept past the struggling horse. The thing dragging Flavio heard him and raised its head. Fargo fired, and in the flash of his Colt he had a fleeting impression of baleful eyes and a lot of teeth.

The thing spun and leaped into the forest in a prodigiously long bound that few wolves or dogs could rival. Fargo fired again and started in after it only to be confronted by an inky mass of vegetation. To try and catch it would be futile. Cursing, he reined around.

Alejandro had arrived and vaulted off his mount. Running to his friend, he dropped to his knees. "Flavio! Speak to me!"

Flavio had gone limp but he raised his head and said weakly, "I am alive, Alejandro."

Fargo swung down and gave Alejandro a hand, carefully moving Flavio to the middle of the clearing.

"His right leg, senor," Alejandro gasped.

Fargo had already seen it. Flavio's pants were shredded from the knee down and stained dark. "I'll build a fire," he offered, and went about gathering downed branches and the tinder he'd need. He was out of lucifers but he had a fire steel and flint in his saddlebags. As the flames rose, Alejandro gasped again.

The leg was bad. The beast's fangs had ripped so deep, the bone was exposed. Flavio had lost a horrendous amount of blood.

"Flavio?" Alejandro said, but his friend had passed out.

Untying his bandanna, Fargo applied it to the leg above the knee. His crude tourniquet stopped the blood but Flavio

33

needed immediate attention. "We have to get him to your camp."

"*Si*," Alejandro agreed. "Constanza is our healer. She can sew him up and restore him."

Fargo had seen people die from losing as much blood as Flavio but he didn't say anything. Together they boosted Flavio onto Alejandro's horse and Alejandro climbed up behind him and wrapped his arm around Flavio's waist.

"Wait for me," Fargo said, but Alejandro was already heading down. He forked leather and snatched the reins to Flavio's animal.

From the woods came a growl.

The Colt leaped into his hand and Fargo shifted in the saddle. He saw nothing other than a wall of black but he sensed the thing was close. All he wanted was a clear shot. The seconds dragged into minutes and the growl wasn't repeated. He shoved the Colt into its holster and lit down the mountain. The entire ride to the bottom he had the sensation that he was being followed, but the wolf or hound or whatever it was didn't show itself.

As he started across the valley floor Fargo looked back in the hope of spotting it. It galled him that, twice now, whatever it was had gotten the better of him. He was commencing to take it personal.

Alejandro was well ahead. Fargo tried to overtake him but the sheepherder was flying for his friend's life and reached the encampment first. By the time he came to a halt and dismounted, a crowd had gathered and Constanza was ministering to Flavio. Constanza had slit open the rest of the pant leg with a knife and was probing the deep lacerations with her fingers.

"We must get him into our wagon," she said to Porfiro. "I will need hot water and my needles and cat gut."

"It will be done," Porfiro said.

Nearly all of them drifted toward the leader's wagon. Two exceptions were a frowning malcontent and a friend of his who stalked up and sneered.

"Big help you were, gringo," Carlos declared.

"Go away, boy," Fargo said.

Carlos stayed where he was. "Another of us might die.

And you are supposed to be our great protector, are you not? What do you have to say for yourself?"

"Flavio went up the mountain on his own," Fargo said. "He should have waited for Alejandro and me."

"That is what Alejandro told us," Carlos responded. "But do you want to know what I think?"

"No."

"I'll tell you anyway." Carlos glanced at his companion as if for support. "I think you are a liar, gringo."

"Do you, now."

"I think your grand promise is hot air. I think you are not any better at killing the Hound than we are." Growing bolder, Carlos poked Fargo in the chest. "I think also maybe you are a coward."

"Think again," Fargo said, and slugged him, unleashing an uppercut that smashed the point of Carlos' chin so hard, Fargo nearly broke his hand.

Carlos landed on his back and didn't move.

The friend grabbed for a knife on his right hip but froze at the click of Fargo's Colt.

"I wouldn't."

"You are quick, gringo," the other man said.

"You haven't seen anything yet," Fargo said. "Take that jackass and make yourselves scarce. When he comes to, tell him that if he ever prods me again, I won't be nice like this time."

The man sniffed. "You took him by surprise, that is all. Mark my words. Carlos is not the kind to forgive and forget. When he comes to his senses he will be out for your blood."

11

The morning dawned gray and bleak. More clouds had scuttled in overnight and the day threatened rain.

Fargo was one of the first up. He seldom slept past daybreak. He kindled a fire and put some of his own coffee on and pondered all that had occurred. Something was troubling him.

A wagon door creaked and Constanza emerged. She looked bone-weary. Putting a hand to the small of her back, she arched and stifled a yawn.

"Long night, I take it," Fargo said.

Constanza gave a slight start. "Senor Fargo, I didn't see you there."

"Will he live?"

"*Si*," Constanza said. She came to the fire. "I have seen bites before but never any so gruesome."

"How so?"

"Whatever it is, it has powerful jaws. There are teeth marks on the bone. And it worried the flesh so badly, I had to cut much of it away to forestall infection." Constanza sadly shook her head. "I am afraid Flavio will walk with a limp for the rest of his days."

"At least he's alive."

"There is life and then there is life," Constanza said. "But I take your point." She looked at him. "I also tended to my grandson. Someone hit him and broke a tooth."

"Poor baby," Fargo said.

"He wouldn't tell me who but we both know it was you."

"Your grandson is a pain in the ass," Fargo said.

"Even so, he is still blood of my blood, and I will not permit you to harm him more than you have."

"That's up to him."

"It is in your best interests, too. My advice to you is to ride on."

"I promised your husband I'd go after the Hound."

"He will not hold it against you if you change your mind," Constanza said.

"I'd hold it against me."

"We can't matter that much to you," Constanza argued. "You hardly know us."

"I know Yoana," Fargo said.

"No," Constanza said. "I suspect there is more to it. Confide in me or not, it is your choice." She bent and picked up a cup and filled it. "I am old, senor. I am patient."

"Refresh my memory about something," Fargo said. "How soon after the cowboys showed up did the attacks begin?"

"*Exactamente?*"

"*Si.*"

Constanza had to think about it. "It was three nights after we learned that the Americano vaqueros had come to Hermanos Valley, we first heard the howls."

"Gracias."

"Which is why we suspected they were behind it," Constanza elaborated. "But now you say the Hound has killed their cattle and tried to attack one of them." She sadly sighed. "I don't know what to think anymore. Or could it be that they lied to you?"

"They seemed sincere."

"But it could all be an act?" Constanza pressed him.

"It could," Fargo conceded.

"Then until you prove otherwise, I will continue to place the blame at their feet."

The wagon door opened and out came Alejandro. Shuffling tiredly over, he helped himself to coffee. "Flavio is finally sleeping peacefully," he said to the old woman.

"Good," she said. "He needs rest more than anything."

"His leg," Alejandro said, and closed his eyes and winced. "He will be a cripple, won't he?"

"Perhaps not," Constanza said.

"But you think he will?"

"*Si.*"

"I make this vow," Alejandro solemnly declared. "From this day forth I will not rest until the Hound that did this to him is dead. I swear by all that's holy."

"God does not like for us to swear by Him," Constanza said. "Pick something else to swear by."

"God will do," Alejandro said.

Again the door opened. This time it was Delicia. Despite the clouds and the horror that permeated the very air, she was gorgeous. "*Buenos días.*"

"Did you sleep well, sweet one?" Constanza asked.

"How could I, Grandmother, with all that was going on?" Delicia focused on Fargo. "And you, senor. What will you do this fine day?"

"Go after the Hound," Fargo said.

"With me at his side," Alejandro informed her.

"Didn't you learn anything from what befell Flavio?" Delicia asked.

"*Si,*" Alejandro responded. "I learned that thing must die, and the sooner, the better for us."

"Senor Fargo," Delicia said. "Talk sense into him. Forbid him to accompany you."

"He's a grown man," Fargo said.

"But not a wise one. You, though, have the benefit of having hunted before. Explain the dangers to him."

"I already know them," Alejandro said.

"You will be maimed like Flavio. Or worse."

"Perhaps," Alejandro told her. "But I will be able to hold my head high and not bent low in shame."

"There is no shame for anyone here," Constanza interrupted. "The men have done all they can. That they have not slain this Hound is through no fault of theirs."

"With two of us after the thing," Alejandro insisted, "maybe we will succeed."

Fargo didn't want him to go but held his peace.

"Just remember, you two," Constanza said. "The Hound isn't your only worry."

"It is all I think about," Alejandro said.

"Don't forget that the cowboys have vowed to drive us out. Should they catch you, there is no predicting what they will do. They might shoot you. Or maybe they will tar and feather you, as the gringos are so fond of doing."

"Over my dead body," Fargo said.

12

The clouds darkened during the morning and by noon Fargo was sure they were in for a storm. He and the young sheepherder were on the grassy bench high above the valley, seeking signs. "We should hunt cover if it starts to rain."

"I don't mind being wet, senor," Alejandro said.

They left the bench and climbed. The higher slopes weren't as thick with trees and were dotted with boulders.

"The Hound has to be flesh and blood," Alejandro said at one point. "Yes?"

"What else would it be?"

"Then why can't we find any sign? Why can't we find tracks or droppings?"

"It's canny, this critter," Fargo said.

"Or it is the spawn of hell," Alejandro declared in earnest. "I have heard of such things. My people whisper about them in the night."

"I don't buy that nonsense. Anything that can hurt us, we can hurt. Or kill."

"I hope you are right, senor," Alejandro said. "It is one thing to be up against a wolf or a dog, another to contend with the Devil."

"Keep thinking like that and you'll freeze when the time comes," Fargo warned.

"Do not worry about me. Dog or devil, I will do what must be done."

Just then Fargo spied a dark circle a quarter of a mile or more above them. "Look there," he said, and pointed.

"A cave, you think?"

"Let's find out."

It was a hard climb. Twice Fargo had to dismount and lead the Ovaro by the reins. The last slope was the steepest.

They left their horses tied to a stunted pine and ascended the rest of the way on foot.

"It's a cave!" Alejandro exclaimed.

The opening was five feet across. The ground around it was undisturbed, with not so much as a single print.

Fargo wasn't surprised when he crouched and entered, only to find a lot of dust and an old spider web. The cave barely went in four feet.

"Nothing has ever lived here," Alejandro said, unable to hide his disappointment.

"The spider," Fargo said, with a flick of a finger at the tattered web.

"I had high hopes. I want the beast dead."

"We'll get it sooner or later," Fargo predicted.

"It is the later that bothers me," Alejandro said. "How many more of my people will it kill?"

Fargo had no answer to that. He turned and gazed down at their horses and then out over the valley. From that high up the sheep were white puffy balls. He could see the encampment and the wagons.

"Who is that?" Alejandro asked, and pointed.

On a bluff behind and above the camp was a man on horseback. He was just sitting there, apparently staring down at the sheepherders without being seen.

"It is a cowboy!" Alejandro declared. "He is spying on my people."

"So long as that's all he's doing," Fargo said.

"We must go find out." Alejandro moved out of the cave. "We will confront him."

"Might be best not to," Fargo advised.

"Senor?"

"Spying is harmless. We go after him, it might end in bloodshed."

"So long as the blood is his."

Fargo tried a different tack. "He'll spot us crossing the valley. We won't be able to get close enough."

Alejandro thoughtfully scratched his chin and suddenly brightened. "Not if we circle around from up here. We can get above him and he'll never see us. Are you coming?" He started down, slipping and sliding.

"Hell," Fargo said.

Plenty of timber provided the cover they needed to reach the north end of the valley without being spotted. They climbed higher while continuing to circle until they reached a point several hundred yards above the cowboy on the bluff.

"I told you it would work," Alejandro boasted. "Now we can sneak close." He wedged the Sharps to his shoulder. "If I were a good shot, I would drop him from here."

"No," Fargo said.

"Perdón?"

"No shooting," Fargo said. "We'll talk to him, is all."

"Who are you to say what we do? He and his kind brought the Hound to our valley. He deserves to pay for the horror they have let loose on us."

"Didn't you hear me say that the Hound has killed some of their cows?"

"Their cows?" Alejandro said, and snorted. "What are cows when it has killed three of us?" He paused. "And tell me. Did you see these dead cows with your own eyes, or do you only have their word for it?"

"I didn't see the dead cows," Fargo admitted.

"There you have it," Alejandro declared. "They lied to you, and now they spy on us. I will try and take him alive so Porfiro may question him but if he resists, I will shoot him."

Fargo let him think that until they had stealthily descended to within a hundred yards of the unsuspecting cowboy.

It was Shorty. He had a leg hooked around his saddle horn and looked as bored as a man could be.

Alejandro grinned at Fargo and raised the Sharps. "A little nearer and he is as good as ours."

Fargo drew his Colt and pressed the muzzle to the young sheepherder's ribs. "I'll take that," he said, and wrested the rifle from Alejandro's grasp.

"What are you doing?" Alejandro demanded. He grabbed for the Sharps.

Fargo swung it behind him and cocked the Colt.

Alejandro turned to stone. "Carlos was right," he hissed. "You have been lying to us. You are one of them."

"Carlos is a jackass," Fargo said. He stepped back but kept the Colt level. "Walk ahead of me. Keep your hands where I can see them. And when I tell you to stop, you damn well stop."

"You plan to hand me over to your friends, is that it?"

"Use your head," Fargo said, and gave him a push.

Muttering under his breath, Alejandro complied, his arms out from his sides.

Fargo led the horses. They skirted boulders and trees and avoided a small patch of talus.

Shorty heard them and turned in the saddle. His hand dropped to his six-shooter but he didn't unlimber it. A puzzled expression on his face, he reined his mount around and waited.

Fargo gave Alejandro another push out into the open. "Behave yourself," he warned.

"Go to hell."

Shorty brought his horse over. "You again," he said to Fargo. "Who's your friend?"

"You can go to hell, too, vaquero," Alejandro spat.

Fargo got straight to the point. "What are you doing here?"

"What do you think?" Shorty rejoined. "Griff sent me to keep an eye on the mutton eaters."

"Where is your dog?" Alejandro demanded.

"Ain't got one," Shorty said. "And if you mean that critter that's killed our cows, we figured it belonged to you until Fargo, there, told us different."

"You lie, gringo."

Shorty put his hand on his six-shooter. "Mister, them's fightin' words."

13

Fargo stepped between them. "You'd shoot an unarmed man?"

"Not normally, no," Shorty said. "But if there's anything I hate worse than a pack of sheep lovers, I've yet to come across it."

"Does your boss feel the same way?"

"Mr. Trask? He sure as hell does," Shorty said. "Why, he hates sheepmen worse than he hates Apaches, and it was an Apache that killed his grandpa."

Alejandro bristled and declared, "That is fine, gringo, because we hate your kind as much as you hate us."

"You're not helping matters," Fargo said.

"The thing you need to decide," Shorty told him, "is which side you'll throw in with. Because I can tell you now that if you're friendly with these sheepers, Mr. Trask won't like it. He's liable to have us do to you as he'll have us do to them."

"Which is what, exactly?"

"You need to ask?" Shorty said, and laughed. "When Mr. Trask gives the word, we'll drive them out. Drive you out, too, if you're in their camp."

"This valley is big enough for the two sides to share."

"Hell, mister. The whole blamed world ain't big enough for cows and sheep to mix. Sheep are locusts on the hoof and there's only one way to control locusts."

"Do me a favor," Fargo said. "Ask Trask not to act until he talks to me."

Shorty snorted. "I can ask him, sure, but I can't guarantee he'll agree. And even if he does, talkin' won't do you a lick of good. He has his mind made up."

"Any word on when he'll get here?"

"Soon," Shorty said. He raised his reins. "Enough palaver. Now that this peckerwood knows I'm here, I might as well light a shuck."

"Yes, run," Alejandro said, "or my amigos and I will drag you from that horse and break every bone in your body."

Shorty leaned down, his smile ice. "I can tell you this, wool man. When the killin' does start, it'll be a pleasure to blow out your wick."

"I dare you to try!" Alejandro exclaimed.

For a moment Fargo thought Shorty would draw but all the short puncher did was grunt in disgust and rein around. "Be seein' you, Fargo. Better make up your mind quick. And make it up right. Mr. Trask wants you gone or dead, I'll be first in line to get the job done." He jabbed his spurs.

Alejandro pumped a fist and swore in Spanish.

"That was stupid," Fargo said.

"You heard him," Alejandro hissed. "They hate us. They want us dead. And the feeling is mutual."

Fargo sighed.

"Nothing you say or do can stop our revenge. If you think it can, you might as well get on your horse and leave Hermanos Valley."

Fargo was commencing to think he should, at that. Only he'd given his word to Porfiro. And then there was Delicia. "Get on your horse."

"Mi rifle, por favor?" Alejandro requested, holding out his hand.

"When that cowpoke is out of range and not before."

"You call me *estúpido*," Alejandro said, "but you are a fool."

Neither of them uttered another word until they reached the wagons. By then Shorty was long out of sight. Fargo tossed the Sharps to Alejandro, who glowered at him and went to join a group of young sheepherders huddled by a fire.

Fargo tied the Ovaro behind Porfiro's wagon. He walked around the corner and nearly collided with someone coming the other way.

"I saw you ride up," Delicia said. "How did it go? Or do I even need to ask?"

"Spent half the day riding all over creation," Fargo said, "and didn't accomplish a damn thing."

"Alejandro doesn't look happy."

"That's putting it mildly."

Delicia clasped her hands and smiled demurely. "Would you like some coffee?"

"If it includes your company," Fargo said.

"Do not let it go to your head," she remarked as they strolled to a fire, "but I have been thinking about you all morning."

"You don't say."

Delicia glanced about as if to ensure she couldn't be heard. "You are a good kisser, senor. My instincts tell me you have a lot of experience with the ladies."

"Some," Fargo said, and rubbed his wrist against hers.

Delicia reacted as if a snake had bit her. Jerking her arm away, she whispered, "Be careful, senor. There are some who would be very angry were they to see you making advances."

"Is that what I'm doing?"

"I am serious," Delicia said. "Some of the men might do you harm."

"They'd have to join the line," Fargo said.

14

Along about the middle of the afternoon the storm broke with fierce intensity. For more than an hour the clouds darkened and the wind rose.

Fargo had stripped the Ovaro and placed his saddle and effects under Porfiro's wagon. He had just deposited his saddlebags and was about to swing out from under the wagon and knock on the door when the rain began to come down in sheets. Within seconds the ground and everything else was drenched.

A lithe figure ducked underneath next to him.

"I wondered what was keeping you," Delicia said, sinking to her knees. Water dripped from her hair and trickled down her cheeks and smooth chin.

"We'd better get you inside," Fargo said, and placed his arm over her shoulders.

"No," Delicia said.

"No?"

She nodded at the downpour and her ruby lips quirked in a smile. "What is your hurry? No one can see us."

It was Fargo's turn to smile. The rain was so heavy, visibility was a few feet. It was as if they were in a cocoon—or their own private little room. As much as he would like to indulge, he said, "Are you sure it's smart?"

"Why not?" Delicia sidled closer.

"Your grandfather and grandmother are right above us."

"So? If we are quiet they will never know." Delicia lightly touched her mouth to his neck.

Fargo could think of a better reason; the storm could end as abruptly as it started. But he'd be damned if he'd look a gift horse in the mouth. Facing her, he cupped her chin. "Last chance to come to your senses."

"I am a grown woman, senor," Delicia said, and fused her mouth to his.

46

Her lips were delicate, yet firm. She didn't so much *kiss* him as *devour* him. Her tongue rimmed his mouth and entwined with his. Her breath grew molten. And her body, where he touched her, responded with the taut ardor of a carnal nature too long denied.

Delicia ground against his manhood, her bosom swelling. Her breasts were ripe melons ready to burst from the vine. He cupped one and then the other, and squeezed, and she moaned deep in her velvet throat.

Easing onto his back with his shoulders propped on his saddle, Fargo pulled her to him. She came willingly, hungrily.

Her hands were everywhere, exploring. Her mouth roamed from his face to his neck to his ear.

Fargo liked this gal. She didn't agonize over whether it was wrong or right; she just did it. He lathered her neck and glued his mouth to hers.

Wet drops spattered his hand. Some of the rain was getting under but not enough to matter. He ran a hand through her hair and down her back to the curve of her bottom. He massaged, and pinched, and she wriggled in delight.

"I like that," Delicia breathed huskily.

So did Fargo. He did it again, then slid a hand along her thigh to her knee. She shivered as if she were cold but her body was as hot as lava.

"I like that, too."

Fargo devoted attention to her legs. Each upward motion brought his hand nearer, until finally he covered her, down low.

Delicia bent into a bow and her mouth parted. So did her legs, to grant him easier access. "I have dreamt of you doing that."

Fargo hiked at her dress while kissing and caressing. He was about to undo his belt buckle when a dark shape moved past the wagon. It was there and it was gone. On two legs, so it couldn't be the Hound. Someone was moving about in the rain for some reason.

"Why did you stop?" Delicia asked.

Fargo didn't realize he had. He got her dress up around her waist and tilted his head to appreciate her alluring symmetry. "You're beautiful," he said, and meant it.

47

"I want you." Delicia stretched her full length against him and bit him, hard, on the chin.

Below his waist, Fargo's pants bulged. When she unexpectedly placed her hand on him, he thought he'd explode. She had none of the timidity of her more civilized sisters in cities and towns. Her need was urgent, and immediate.

To Fargo's extreme pleasure, she wore no undergarments.

A twist of his wrist and he was there. Her slit was wet with her yearning. He stroked, lightly, and she stifled a groan.

"I have never wanted anyone as much as I want you."

Fargo kept one ear primed to the rain. The storm continued in all its elemental fury, with no sign of relenting, which suited him just fine.

Delicia lived up to her name. From her soft lips to her smooth thighs, she was exquisite. Her hands were all over him.

When he slid a finger into her, she thrust with her hips, the friction adding heat where they were already burning.

Fargo hiked her dress higher to expose her globes. As her melons fell free, he inhaled a nipple and sucked. She cooed and wriggled. He nipped lightly with the tip of his teeth, and she shuddered. He cupped and pulled and she sank her teeth into his shoulder.

Petting, kneading, lips locked, their breaths became furnace pants of pure desire. When, at length, he inserted the tip of his manhood, she looked into his eyes and whispered, "*Si*. Oh, *si*."

Fargo penetrated her. Delicia's face became a mirror of ecstasy. She threw her head back and nearly bumped it on the bottom of the wagon. She did more grinding, matching her rhythm to his.

Above and around them the rain pelted the world. In their own little shelter, they drifted on the rising tides of mutual pleasure until, with her next impalement, Delicia gushed. She came and she came, and at the height of her release, Fargo went over the brink.

In inner free fall from the heights, Fargo happened to glance at the rear of the wagon and for a fleeting instant he swore that he saw a pair of legs and boots. They were there and they were gone. As Delicia collapsed on top of him, he placed his hand on his Colt.

"You are a magnificent lover," she whispered.

Fargo was watching for the legs to reappear. When they didn't, he let himself relax.

Delicia kissed his chin. "Thank goodness for the storm, eh? I hope we can do this again soon."

"You and me, both," Fargo said.

15

The tempest lasted another hour. By then they had put themselves together, and as soon as the rain slackened enough that she wouldn't be soaked, Delicia pecked Fargo on the cheek and darted out from under the wagon.

The rear door opened and closed.

Fargo was one of the first to emerge after the last few drops fell. The Ovaro, and everything else, was dripping wet.

The fires were black circles. Dozens of nearby sheep looked miserable.

Fargo decided to rekindle a fire and put coffee on. Firewood was kept in a box attached to the side of the wagon, and he was opening it when the squish of a stealthy footstep gave him a split-second's warning. He turned, and a steel blade bit into the box instead of between his shoulder blades.

"Bastardo!" Carlos hissed. Spinning on the balls of his feet, he cut at Fargo's neck.

Ducking, Fargo backpedaled.

"I know what you did with my *hermana*," Carlos snarled, and came at him like a madman.

Fargo did more backpedaling. He didn't want to kill him if he could help it but he might not be able to. He skipped aside, avoiding a stab at his chest, grabbed Carlos' wrist, and wrenched. His intent was to disarm him but Carlos not only held on to the knife, he kicked at his knee. Fargo managed to shift so that his shin took the blow but it still hurt like hell and he stumbled and nearly fell.

"I will kill you, gringo!"

Fargo smashed his fist into the young sheepherder's jaw.

The blow rocked Carlos onto his heels but he was tougher than he looked and didn't go down. Hooking a foot behind him, Fargo tripped him and slammed him onto his back. As they crashed down Fargo contrived to ram his knee into Carlos' gut. It had the desired effect—Carlos cried out, and his knife arm went slack.

Fargo slugged him, and Carlos went limp.

"What is the meaning of this?"

It was Porfiro.

Fargo stood and stepped back. "I reckon your grandson isn't too fond of me."

Porfiro squatted and plucked the knife from the wet grass.

"My grandson has always had a bad temper. What set him off?"

"You'd have to ask him," Fargo hedged. To admit the truth might get Delicia in trouble.

"I napped during the storm," Porfiro said. "Constanza just woke me and I came out to see how you were. You should have come inside with us where it is dry."

"I was fine out here."

Porfiro looked down in disappointment at the fruit of his family's loins. "I am sorry, Senor Fargo. This was no way to treat a guest in our camp."

"Forget it."

"How can I? He shames us with his behavior." Porfiro gave a shake of his head. "But we have other matters to discuss, do we not?"

"The cowboys."

"*Si*," Porfiro said. "Alejandro has told me what the vaquero said about this man called Trask, and how he hates our kind. It does not bode well."

"No," Fargo agreed. "It doesn't."

"It is not enough we have the Hound to deal with," Porfiro said. "What have we done that God inflicts so many difficulties on us?"

"I'm no parson," Fargo said.

"I am worried, senor. My people mean more to me than the breath of life. I have led them for more than twenty years, and I think of them as my children."

"You're a good man, Porfiro."

"Not good enough or I would have solutions to our problems. The beast kills us, the cowboys say they want to kill us." The old sheepherder closed his eyes and rubbed his brow. "I am afraid I am not equal to the task of protecting those I care for."

"You're doing all you can."

"It's not enough, senor." Porfiro looked at Fargo, his eyes haunted by the prospect of the possible horrors to come. "Advise me, senor. Help me help my people."

Before Fargo could reply, hooves drummed and two of the men who had gone out with guns were back.

"The sheep!" one of them exclaimed. "So many sheep!"

The other one nodded and crossed himself.

"Calm down, Lorenzo," Porfiro said to the first. "What has happened?"

"You must see for yourself," Lorenzo said.

"We sought shelter from the rain in the woods," the other man related. "When the storm was over we resumed our hunt for the Hound, and that is when we found them."

"Come," Lorenzo said. *"Rapidamente."*

"I must saddle my horse," Porfiro said.

"I'll tag along," Fargo offered.

In ten minutes the four of them were galloping hard to the southwest. Sheep were everywhere.

Presently they came to a rocky spine Fargo had passed on his way to the cowboy camp. A hundred yards farther was another. Fargo remembered seeing a lot of sheep in the horseshoe-shaped area in between when he was on his way to visit the cowboys.

"Brace yourselves," Lorenzo warned.

16

The sheep Fargo had seen were still there. Sixty or seventy, by his reckoning—and all of them dead.

"God in heaven!" Porfiro cried, aghast.

They lay singly or in clusters, most with their throats torn out, more than a few with their bellies ripped open and their intestines in coils on the grass. They were still wet from the rain, and much of the blood had been washed into the earth.

Dismounting, Porfiro stumbled to a ewe, dropped to his knees, and clasped its head in his hands. "Our poor babies. Why didn't they run? Why did they let themselves be slaughtered?"

Fargo thought he had the answer. "It came on them in the storm."

"And they couldn't hear or see it until it was too late?" Porfiro nodded. "Yes, that makes sense." He gestured. "But how could one animal kill so many? I have seen mountain lions kill two or three, but this—" He had no words.

Fargo had heard tell of similar frenzies. In New Mexico once, a mountain lion killed upward of twenty. And in Arizona a big cat got into a sheep pen and tore apart thirty or more. He mentioned the attacks to Porfiro.

"But this wasn't a lion, senor. It was the Hound. Dogs do not do such a thing."

"It is more than a dog," Lorenzo said. "It is a devil."

"A demon," said the other man.

"Here we go again," Fargo said.

"Do not talk nonsense," Porfiro chided them. "We have heard it. Senor Fargo has seen it. It is flesh and blood, like any animal, and like any animal, it can be killed."

"If you say so," Lorenzo said dubiously.

Porfiro gently lowered the ewe's head, and stood. "We must salvage what we can of the wool and the meat. Go back to camp and bring the others."

"What about you?" Lorenzo asked.

"I will stay with Fargo and look for sign."

Fargo was already searching. He threaded among the bodies, bent low. Thanks to the storm, there wasn't any sign to find. The rain had washed away the few prints the Hound may have left. He drew rein at the tree line and stared off up the mountain wondering where the beast had gotten to.

"Why have you stopped?" Porfiro asked. "We must hunt it down while there is daylight left."

"We can't find it if there aren't any tracks," Fargo said. But he gigged the stallion and climbed anyway. Twenty feet up stood a number of small spruce, their branches close together. He went to go around and drew rein, instead. Swinging down, he dropped to a knee.

"What have you found?"

"See for yourself."

In a patch of bare earth was a print. Just one, but it was complete and clear and left no doubt as to its maker's identity.

"Madre de Dios," Porfiro said in amazement.

Fargo didn't blame him. The track was eight inches from end to end, and nearly as wide as it was long. He whistled to himself. In the geyser country a few years ago he and some others came across wolf tracks six inches long, and they were considered gigantic. Eight inches was unheard of.

"What is it, senor?" Porfiro asked. "A dog or a wolf? You can tell by the track, can you not?"

"Usually," Fargo said.

"What are you saying?"

"Dog and wolves have four toes, the same as coyotes and foxes," Fargo began. "On dogs the inner two are closer together than on a wolf."

Porfiro intently studied the track. "I can stick my thumb in the space between the inner two on this one. So it must be a wolf, yes?"

"If that was all we had to go by," Fargo said. "But the shape isn't like any wolf track I've ever seen."

"It is neither a dog *nor* wolf? How can that be?"

"It can't," Fargo said, and confessed, "I don't know what the hell it is."

"I don't understand," Porfiro said.

"Makes two of us." Fargo moved in among the spruce and found a partial print of a rear paw. Like the front, it was gigantic. Like the front, it seemed to suggest that the animal wasn't wolf or dog.

"We must keep this to ourselves," Porfiro said at Fargo's shoulder. "My people are superstitious. Some already believe the beast is a demon, as you heard with your own ears. Should they learn that a seasoned scout and tracker like yourself can't tell what it is, there will be a panic."

"If it leaves tracks, it's real," Fargo said.

"I agree. So again, I beg you, do not say one word of this to anyone else. Do you promise?"

Fargo nodded.

"Gracias."

Suddenly wheeling, Fargo made for the Ovaro. "I'm a damned dunderhead."

"Senor?"

"That track was made *after* the storm. Which means the Hound or whatever the hell it is can't have more than a half-hour start." Fargo quickly climbed on. "Stay here and wait for Lorenzo and the rest. I don't know when I'll be back."

"Senor, wait . . ."

Fargo didn't linger. Twin pricks of his spurs, and he climbed swiftly. The rain had softened the soil enough that there were plenty of tracks. At last luck favored him. He'd be able to follow the beast for miles, possibly even to its lair.

In no time Fargo reached the grassy bench. He crested the rim, and swore.

More dead sheep were scattered willy-nilly, in the same state as their slaughtered brethren below.

Fargo stopped counting at fifteen. He crossed the bench and found more prints leading higher. It helped that the clouds were breaking and the sky was clearing. With six or seven hours of daylight left, he was confident he could catch the creature before sundown.

Shucking the Henry, Fargo held it across his saddle. He may get only one shot, and have only seconds in which to get it off. He must be ready.

No sooner did the thought cross his mind than he glanced up and spotted . . . something . . . staring down at him.

55

17

The animal was on its haunches. That much alone told Fargo it wasn't a deer. Its color was grayish-brown.

Fargo raised the Henry to his shoulder but he didn't shoot. The thing was on a rocky ridge hundreds of yards higher, well out of range. Snapping the rifle down, he goaded the Ovaro.

The animal sat watching him. Just when he was close enough to try a shot, it turned and melted from view.

He chalked it up to coincidence—or was it?

After a few minutes Fargo attained the crest. Tracks confirmed it was indeed the beast, and that the four-legged killer had gone off up the mountain.

"You're not losing me that easy," Fargo vowed.

Presently he came to a field of boulders. They were a virtual maze. Some were so large he couldn't see over them.

And the beast was in among them.

Fargo was tempted to rein around and get out of there but there wasn't room to turn the stallion. He went in ever deeper, his thumb on the Henry's hammer, his forefinger curled around the trigger.

The tracks were plain enough. Then, suddenly, they weren't there.

Fargo realized the animal had gone into an intersecting gap and he'd missed it. Now the thing could be anywhere.

It occurred to him that he could lure the beast in by just sitting there. The only way to come at him was from the front and the rear, and by shifting in the saddle he could keep an eye in both directions.

Time passed. A raven flapped overhead. Somewhere sparrows were chirping.

Fargo stayed still. So did the Ovaro save for the occasional swish of its tail.

This was the hardest part of hunting—the waiting. Good

hunters must possess extraordinary patience, and he was widely considered one of the best. Once he'd sat motionless in a tree for eleven hours to shoot a grizzly. Another time, he'd roosted cross-legged for so long, waiting for an elk, that when he tried to stand his legs wouldn't work.

A pebble clattered and Fargo tensed. It came from in front of him. Thumbing the hammer, he put his cheek to the rifle.

A gap between boulders grew dark with shadow. The beast growled but didn't show itself.

All Fargo wanted was for it to poke its head out. He held his breath to steady his aim.

The thing sniffed, loudly, a few times. It growled again, and the shadow disappeared.

Fargo swore and gigged the Ovaro. He reached the gap and centered the Henry but the thing was gone. The opening wasn't wide enough for the stallion. He was forced to take a long way around, and it was a good twenty minutes before he emerged from the boulder field close to a rise. He couldn't find tracks. He scanned the surrounding area. Nothing.

"Damn it to hell."

Fargo refused to give up. He went completely around the boulders, and still no tracks. Either the thing was still in there or it had made its escape along patches of rocky ground.

Once again Fargo had been thwarted. He let down the hammer and shoved the Henry into the saddle scabbard.

All the way down to the bench he kept hoping for another glimpse but it wasn't to be.

Porfiro and several others had found the second bunch of dead sheep and were salvaging what they could. One look at Fargo's face and Porfiro said, "No need to say anything. I can tell you were not successful."

"The damn thing must be Irish," Fargo said.

"Senor?"

"Nothing." Fargo swung a leg over and slid off. "Its luck can't hold forever. Sooner or later I'll put a slug in its brainpan."

"It is the latter that worries me," Porfiro said. "We have lost nearly sixty sheep in one afternoon. Imagine if the beast goes on other killing sprees. We could lose hundreds before it is dead."

"I'm doing the best I can."

"I don't doubt that for a minute," Porfiro assured him. "Believe me when I say I am sincerely grateful for all you have done. I wish the cowboys were more like you."

Hooves drummed, and onto the bench galloped Delicia. "Grandfather!" she cried. She swept by the men working on the sheep and was off her horse before it stopped moving. "You must come quickly."

"What now?" Porfiro wearily asked.

"It is Carlos and Alejandro," Delicia said. "They saw the dead sheep below and were enraged. They say it is a dog that did this, and that the dog belongs to the cowboys."

"We do not have proof of that."

"They don't care. They have gone to punish the cowboys for the dead sheep."

"God, no," Porfiro said.

"I tried to talk them out of it. Lorenzo, too. He urged them to speak to you first."

"Good for Lorenzo."

"Carlos almost hit him. My brother was practically beside himself. I have never seen him so mad. And Alejandro was little better. He is upset over Flavio."

"Carlo and Alejandro have hot blood, those two," Porfiro said. "They have always been too quick to anger."

"I begged Carlos not to go but he pushed me aside," Delicia said. "He has never laid a hand on me before."

"He will regret it when he comes to his senses."

Delicia didn't seem to hear him. "Then they rode off, Grandfather, taking rifles with them, and I came to find you."

"The fools," Porfiro said. "They will bring ruin down on our heads."

"Not if I can help it," Fargo said. He was back in the saddle, and away.

Delicia shouted for him to wait for her but he wasn't about to.

Fargo crossed the bench and started down. On the valley floor, a mile or more distant, two riders were trotting to the south.

Fargo had a long, hard ride ahead. Unless he stopped them, the pair would ignite a bloodbath that would turn Hermanos Valley red.

18

There were times when even Skye Fargo marveled at the Ovaro's stamina. This was one of them. He reached the bottom and for over two miles flew in pursuit. But Carlos and Alejandro had too great a lead. Eventually, reluctantly, he slowed to a walk to spare the stallion from exhaustion.

Seven of the eleven miles were behind him when a shot echoed off the surrounding peaks. A second blast thundered on the heels of the first.

Fargo imagined the worst—that the pair had killed a cowboy. It turned out they hadn't, but they had done something almost as bad. In half a mile he came on two cows; blood and brains were oozing from holes in the skulls, and flies were gathering.

With newfound urgency Fargo hastened on. The punchers were bound to have heard the shots and would investigate.

Around the next bend was a straight stretch. At the far end, brazenly riding down the middle of the valley, were Carlos and Alejandro.

Fargo urged the stallion into a trot. They heard him and looked around and stopped. Aware that at any moment the cowboys might appear, he vented his anger the moment he drew rein. "What in hell do you think you're doing?"

Carlos and Alejandro swapped smirks.

"You saw the cows, did you not?" Carlos said.

"We killed them to show these gringos they can't kill our sheep with impunity," Alejandro boasted.

"Jackasses," Fargo said. "The both of you."

Alejandro bristled with resentment. "We won't have you insult us."

"No, we will not," Carlos said. "You're not one of us. You are a gringo yourself, so naturally you take the side of those who would drive us out."

Fargo controlled his temper with an effort. "I haven't taken anyone's side, and you damn well know it."

"We do not want you here," Alejandro said. "It is Porfiro who likes you and allows you to stay with us."

"Do us a favor, gringo," Carlos said. "Go away and leave us to our fight."

"They'll kill you for the cows," Fargo said.

Carlos snorted and patted his rifle. "Let them try. They will find that we are men and men are not afraid to die."

"They want to drive us from our valley but it is they who will go," Alejandro said.

"This is Porfiro's fault," Carlos said. "We should have confronted them the day we discovered they were here but he persuaded us not to."

"He bends over backwards to be civil," Alejandro threw in. "And now three of us are dead, and a lot of our sheep, besides."

"No more," Carlos said. "Today we show them that we are not cowards."

"Are you done preening?" Fargo said. "There are eight of them and two of you."

"Soon there will be less of them."

"Idiots," Fargo said.

"You have delayed us long enough," Carlos declared. He nodded at Alejandro and they continued to the south.

Fargo quickly caught up. "Listen to me." He tried one last appeal. "If you're smart, you'll make yourselves scarce before the Texans find those dead cows."

"Enough with the cows," Alejandro said.

"Tiene vacas en el cerebro," Carlos said, and both of them laughed.

They neared the next bend. From around the other side rumbled the thud of hooves.

"They're coming," Fargo said the obvious.

"Good." Alejandro wedged his rifle to his shoulder. "Now we repay them for Ramon and the others."

In disgust Fargo reined to the west. He'd tried to talk sense into them and they'd thrown it in his face. The consequences were on their heads. He would go into the trees and swing north and let Porfiro know that he had done all he could.

Sooner than he expected the cowboys swept into sight, all eight, with Griff Wexler in the lead.

Fargo glanced over his shoulder to see what the sheepherders would do. They weren't there. Their horses were, but Carlos and Alejandro had climbed down and were lying in the grass. He opened his mouth to shout a warning but it was too late.

Their rifles boomed and a cowboy swayed in the saddle. Instantly the rest grabbed for their six-shooters and Griff Wexler bawled for them to hunt cover.

Three of the cowboys reined in the same direction Fargo had gone. They saw him—and opened fire.

Fargo got out of there. It wouldn't do any good to try to explain that he wasn't part of this. Leaden hornets buzzed his head as he slapped his legs.

The three came after him.

Fargo was furious. Furious at himself, not at the cowboys. This was what he got for trying to play peacemaker. He should have lit a shuck days ago.

A shot nicked his hat.

Bending low over the saddle horn, Fargo flew for his life. He cursed all sheep and those who tended them and all cows and those who rode herd.

Behind him more rifles and pistols blasted.

The cowboys had opened up on the sheepherders.

Yet another slug chipped a tree as Fargo plunged into the woods. He climbed a dozen yards and reined around, drawing the Colt as he turned.

The three punchers burst in after him and one jerked his pistol up.

Fargo shot him. He aimed at the man's shoulder but the man shifted just as he squeezed the trigger and he was sure the slug hit lower. "Drop your hardware!" he bellowed at the other two.

Instead of obeying one veered to the right and the other to the left.

Fargo swung behind an oak. It wasn't much cover but he hoped it would cause them to break away and hunt cover of their own.

It didn't.

Yipping like Apaches, the two Texans closed on him, their six-guns blazing.

Slivers exploded from the oak and several stung Fargo's face. He aimed at the rider on the right, and fired. This time he didn't try for the shoulder; he shot dead-center and the man's arms flew back and his legs flew up and he tumbled over the back of his saddle.

A slug clipped a whang on Fargo's buckskins.

The other cowboy was almost on him. Swiveling, he stroked the trigger. The cowboy twisted to the impact, recovered, and brought his six-shooter to bear.

Fargo shot him in the head. The cowboy's hat went flying, as did a goodly portion of his hair and brains. His body fell hard and the dun galloped past the Ovaro and off into the forest.

Mad as hell, Fargo climbed the mountain to a flat knob.

The valley was quiet now, the valley floor still. A horse stood by itself in the grass. Nearby lay a prone figure but Fargo couldn't tell who it was. To the north a lone rider was fleeing.

Fargo reloaded. He had a choice to make. He could ride north, too, even though this wasn't his fight, or he could circle to the south and be shed of Hermanos Valley.

Fargo frowned. When he'd offered to hunt the Hound, he had no intention of becoming involved in a range war. If he went north he would be, whether he wanted to or not.

"Damn," he said, and reined north.

The fleeing rider covered three miles before his horse gave out. The animal was lathered with sweat and stumbling when Fargo emerged from the timber. The man on the horse was swearing and kicking it and didn't hear him come up.

"It would be you," Fargo said.

Carlos jerked his head up. "You!" he exclaimed. "I saw you run off, coward."

Fargo came alongside the exhausted bay. "Because of you I had to kill two cowpokes."

"You did? That is excellent."

"Not for them," Fargo said, and backhanded him across the face. He didn't hold back. He used his fist and slammed it hard.

Carlos squawked as he pitched from the saddle. He landed on his shoulder and lost his hold on his rifle. With a cry of rage he pumped to his hands and knees and scrambled to retrieve it.

Fargo was already off the Ovaro. He took two steps and kicked Carlos in the side. The blow flipped him onto his back and he lay clutching himself and swearing.

"Why did you do that?"

"I'll say it again," Fargo said. "I had to kill two of them, and you're to blame." He kicked Carlos in the leg and Carlos whimpered and slid out of reach.

"Stop! It's not my fault. They started it. Be mad at them, not at me."

Fargo stalked toward him. "Do you have any idea what you've done, you miserable son of a bitch?"

Fear on his face, Carlos cried, "Beat me if it will make you feel better but I did what I had to and I have no regrets." He pushed to his knees. "My people will be proud of what I have done."

"Aren't you forgetting someone?"

"Eh?" Carlos straightened. "Oh. You mean Alejandro? The gringo you call Shorty shot him. So it is four of us they have killed now, and not three."

"Too bad it's not five," Fargo said, and drawing his Colt, he slashed the barrel across Carlos' temple.

Without a sound, Carlos pitched forward.

Fargo climbed on the Ovaro before temptation got the better of him. He left Carlos lying there, grabbed the reins to the bay, and in half an hour was in sight of the sheepherder's wagons.

Constanza came to meet him, a shawl over her head and shoulders. "That is the horse my grandson was riding. Where is he?"

"He should be along in an hour or so," Fargo said, alighting. "I can't say the same for Alejandro."

"What has happened?"

Fargo kept it brief. He omitted the part about knocking Carlos senseless. He figured she would be as angry as he was about the dead cowboys but he was wrong.

"My grandson has done fine," Constanza said happily. "At last we have drawn blood."

"It's nothing to crow about," Fargo said.

"Ah, but it is, senor. The gringos will think twice before they bother us again."

"You think too little of them."

"And you think too much. They are greedy men with no regard for others. Carlos has shown them that we will not be pushed around."

"Remind me of that when their whole outfit swoops down on you."

"I most assuredly will. I'm not afraid of them."

"I see where Carlos gets it from," Fargo said.

"Gets what? His dislike for gringos?" Constanza nodded. "His father—my son—is also a lot like me. It is a shame he isn't here. He took his wife for supplies before all this started and won't be back for a week to ten days."

"He'll miss all the killing," Fargo said.

"*Si*," Constanza said. "It is a shame."

20

More dark clouds scuttled in from the west, the second thunderhead in as many days.

The sky matched Fargo's mood. Hunkered by a fire with a cup of coffee in his hands, he sipped and pondered the comments he'd heard over the past hour.

Somehow he'd gotten it into his head that sheepherders were peaceful, meek folk. Not this bunch. The deaths and the sheep kills had riled them to where they were ready to "wipe out the gringos," as one man put it.

He had to wonder if they had any notion of what they were up against. Cowboys, especially the Texas breed, weren't known for turning the other cheek. They were hard as nails and tough as leather and woe to anyone who made trouble for their brand.

A horse approached from the south bearing two people. Delicia was the rider; Carlos was behind her. She drew rein at the horse string and tied off her animal. Carlos made for his grandparents' wagon but she gazed about, spied Fargo, and stalked over.

"How could you?" she angrily demanded.

"It's good coffee," Fargo said.

"I am talking about my brother. You beat Carlos so bad, his face is swollen."

"He's still breathing."

Delicia squatted so they were face-to-face. "How can you be so callous? I thought you and I were friends, possibly even more than friends."

Fargo admired the color in her cheeks and how her eyes flashed. "Did he tell you what he did?"

"About shooting the two cows? And one of the cowboys? So what? We have paid them back for the sheep they killed."

"Cowboys don't generally use their teeth to kill things," Fargo said. "And I expected better of you."

"It is us against them."

"So you're proud of the bastard, too?"

"My brother? *Si*."

"I was wrong," Fargo said. "Carlos isn't the jackass. I am."

"You're not making any sense," Delicia said. "The important thing is that the cowboys have said they want our valley for their own. That we can not allow."

"And Alejandro?"

"What about him? Carlos says he died bravely, fighting on our behalf."

"It will get ugly now," Fargo said. "A lot more of you will die."

"A lot of them will die, too."

"You're a bloodthirsty wench," Fargo said, and he wasn't smiling.

"Surely you can't blame me for siding with my own people? I would die for them, as I would die for the right to graze our sheep where we have grazed them for hundreds of years."

"It may come to that."

"Are you trying to scare me? Is that it?"

"A little fear could keep you alive."

"What kind of talk is that?" Delicia snapped. "Why should I fear cowboys? They are men. Common, ordinary men. And Carlos says there are only a few left now."

"Their boss is due any day," Fargo said. "They'll have more guns than you, more horses."

"We'll have right on our side."

"Hell," Fargo said.

"You take us too lightly," Delicia said. "As I suspect the cowboys do. That is their mistake."

"Listen to yourself."

"Are *you* listening?" Delicia countered.

"Your people tend sheep, for God's sake."

"And they tend cows. Explain to me how that means they are better than us?"

"They are better with guns," Fargo said, growing angry himself. "And you can't fight guns with good intentions."

Delicia went to say more but looked up as several riders approached from the northwest. "Grandfather," she said, and rose.

Everyone gathered to meet him. Everyone except Fargo. He stayed by the fire, happy to be ignored.

Questions were shouted at Porfiro. How many sheep had been slain, in all? Fifty-four. Where were the rest of the men? Bringing the meat and the wool. Did they see the Hound? No, they did not.

Constanza, Delicia and Carlos took Porfiro aside. Their talk became heated. Porfiro jabbed a finger at Carlos and Carlos stomped off in a huff.

Fargo wasn't surprised when the old man broke away and came straight to him.

"I need advice, senor."

"Leave," Fargo said.

"The valley? No. We can't."

"Then die."

"Hear me out, *por favor*. You tried to stop my grandson, and for that I am grateful. But we have reached the point where there is no turning back." Porfiro held out his hands in appeal. "What do I do? How can I stop more blood from being spilled?"

"You can't."

"There must be something."

"Leave," Fargo said again. "Pack up your wagons and gather up your sheep and get the hell out of here while you still can."

"Have you no other advice than that?"

"Dig a lot of graves," Fargo said.

21

When it happened it wasn't as Fargo expected.

The next morning the sheepherders were sitting around after breakfast debating how best to prepare for the cowboys when a lone rider was spotted coming up the valley at a trot.

It was Shorty.

Fargo had to hand it to him. After all that had happened, for the puncher to come to the sheepherder camp alone took a lot of sand.

Shorty was leading a horse with a body over it. He boldly rode up and leaned on his saddle horn and said pleasantly, "Mornin', folks."

"*Buenos días*, senor," Porfiro said.

"You speak English, hoss?" Shorty said. "My Spanish lingo is a mite rusty."

"I speak good English, yes. What may we do for you?"

"I believe this is yours," Shorty said, and turning, he tugged the other horse up next to his.

The body was Alejandro's.

"We thank you," Porfiro said. "We were afraid the coyotes and vultures would have been at it by now."

Carlos took a step, his face livid, his mouth working with suppressed fury. "*Bastardo!* You brought him back to rub our noses in his death."

"Carlos, no," Porfiro said.

Whirling, Carlos shook his rifle at him. "Why are you being so civil to this pig? He and his kind are out to kill us or drive us off and you talk to him as if you are the best of friends."

Constanza moved between them and placed a hand on Carlos' chest. "Let your grandfather handle this, for now. The cowboy did not come all this way just to return the body."

"No, ma'am," Shorty said. "I surely didn't. Mr. Trask sent me with a message."

"Your employer?" Porfiro said. "He has come at last?"

Shorty nodded. "And he aims to set things right. He sent the body as a token of good will, as he called it. And he wants me to extend an invite to him." Shorty pointed at Fargo. "He'd like for you to come for supper. About sundown will do."

Fargo was as surprised as the sheepherders. "Why me?"

"We told him how you took their side. He wants to make everything plain to you and you can make it plain to these sheepers."

"Why not just invite some of them?"

"Mr. Trask wants you. What do I tell him? Will you be there or not?"

Before Fargo could answer, Porfiro turned to him.

"We would be grateful if you went on our behalf. If there is a chance we can work out our differences, we must try."

"I only stuck around to hunt the Hound," Fargo said. And to make love to Delicia, but he kept that to himself.

"That damn thing killed six more of our cows last night," Shorty remarked.

"What?" Porfiro was startled. "It killed over fifty of our sheep just yesterday."

"Fifty?" Shorty cocked his head. "For real?"

"He's telling the truth," Fargo confirmed.

"Well, now. This will interest Mr. Trask. It can't hardly be your critter if it's killin' your woollies." Shorty raised his reins. "Will you come or not?"

"I'll be there," Fargo said.

Shorty grunted and rode off.

"No," Carlos snarled, and tried to raise his rifle but Constanza gripped the barrel and shook her head.

"Now is not the time."

Porfiro was smiling. "I am encouraged. It was considerate of this Trask to give us Alejandro so we can bury him. Perhaps he is not the heartless brute some of us believed him to be."

"Don't count your chickens before they're hatched," Fargo said.

"Chickens, senor? We raise sheep."

"It's a saying." Fargo didn't elaborate. He was watching Shorty, and wondering.

Delicia had been quiet the whole time but now she stepped forward and announced, "I am going for a ride. Would someone like to go with me?" She looked at Fargo.

"I would," Lorenzo offered.

"I suppose I could go," Carlos said, not sounding happy about the idea.

Some of the other young men smiled hopefully.

"How about you, senor?" Delicia bluntly asked Fargo.

"Where are you riding to?"

"To check on the sheep," Delicia said.

"That is man's work," Carlos told her.

Delicia ignored him. "Will you come or not? If we find sign of the beast, you are the best tracker. And you did say it is why you have stuck around."

"You made up my mind. I'll tag along."

"I thought you might," Delicia said.

She led him to the horse string, her backside, Fargo thought, swaying more than was usual. As they were throwing their saddles on she looked over her sorrel at him and said quietly, "There is another reason I asked you to come. Can you guess what it is?"

"Does it involve you naked?"

Delicia grinned. "It could."

22

They rode to the north, into the forest and up several slopes to a patch of woods with a clearing in the middle.

Delicia drew rein and slid down. She stretched, her bosom outlined against her dress, and bestowed a sultry smile. "Are you pleased?"

"Lorenzo and some of the others will be hankering to shoot me," Fargo said.

"I'm a grown woman, senor. I can be with who I want. They have no say."

"You're also the prettiest woman in the whole camp," Fargo said. "You can't hardly blame them for wanting to stake a claim."

"I am not their property," Delicia said, and brightened. "Am I really the prettiest? You did not say that just to flatter me?"

"The prettiest by far." Fargo led their horses to a tree and tied them. He peered down the mountain but didn't see anyone on their back trail. He yanked the Henry from the saddle scabbard anyway. When he returned to the middle of the clearing, she was sitting with her legs out and her arms propped behind her.

"Have a seat, handsome one," Delicia said, patting the ground beside her.

"Don't mind if I do." Fargo sat and leaned his own arms back. He was in no hurry.

"What do you think this Trask is up to?"

"Who knows?" Fargo touched her leg and smiled. "I thought you invited me up here for something besides more talk."

"I did, but I am worried," Delicia said. "It was noble of you to agree to go on our behalf. You can find out how many men he has with him, and how many guns."

71

"They're Texans," Fargo said.

"What does that mean?"

"They'll all have guns. They may not use them all that well but they'll have them."

"Not use them well?" Delicia said skeptically.

"Few cowpokes are gun hands," Fargo explained. "They shoot snakes and such, and raise hell when they go into a town on a spree. But they don't practice a lot, and most are only fair shots, at best."

"So you are saying we have little to fear?"

"I didn't say that at all," Fargo said to set her straight. "I don't know how many hands Trask brought, but twenty or thirty cowboys with guns is a hell of a lot more than five or six sheepherders with guns."

Delicia bit her lower lip. "I hope you can convince this Trask to be reasonable."

"When it comes to their cows, ranchers are downright touchy," Fargo enlightened her. "If he has his sights set on Hermanos Valley, I can talk myself blue in the face and he won't listen."

Delicia sighed. "Between the cowboys and the Hound, our lives have become a nightmare."

Fargo didn't tell her that he expected it to get a lot worse before it got better.

"Four of us have died. And so many sheep. And our dogs before that," Delicia said sadly.

Fargo looked up. "Dogs?"

"Sheepherders always have dogs, senor. We had six of the finest. They were the first things the Hound killed."

"No one mentioned them before."

"It didn't come up. When they disappeared we thought maybe a mountain lion was to blame. Then we heard the howls and realized it was something else."

"I wish someone had told me this."

"That is another reason my father and mother left. To bring back new dogs. If they can find some that can be trained, that is."

Fargo mulled this latest revelation. It strengthened the hunch he had. Proving it would take some doing, though. He realized Delicia had gone on and focused on her.

". . . can't use just any dog. It is best if they are bred to the wool, as we like to say. Unfortunately, good sheepdogs are hard to find."

"Enough about dogs," Fargo said, and traced a finger from her shoulder to her elbow.

"Typical man," Delicia said. "Always with one thing on your mind."

"Whiskey?"

Delicia laughed. "I would love to spend a night in town with you. Any town. I would wear the best dress I have, and we could dine, and dance, and have a wonderful time."

"We can have a wonderful time right here."

"You have no romance, senor," Delicia said, but not unkindly.

"I could go pick some flowers if it will put you in the mood."

"The thing that will put me in the mood," Delicia said, "is if you ravish me."

"That I can do," Fargo said.

23

Fargo kissed her. Delicia's mouth parted and her tongue met his. After a while he put his arm around her and lowered her onto her back. Stretching out, he pressed his chest to hers and kissed and licked her throat and ears. She cooed softly.

Removing his hat, she ran her fingers through his hair and over his shoulders.

Fargo covered her left breast with his hand and squeezed. Delicia wriggled, nipped his earlobe, arched. He felt her nipple harden under his palm. She raised her right thigh and rubbed it against his leg.

Fargo was going to cup her bottom but she suddenly pushed him onto his back and slid on top of him. Breathing into his ear, she grinned and said huskily, "Relax and enjoy."

Delicia lavished wet kisses on his lips and cheeks and neck while rubbing her body against his. Her mouth, her body, were hotter by the moment.

Fargo felt a tight sensation as his bulge tried to burst from his pants.

Delicia felt it, too. Grinning, she said, "What do we have here?" and placed her hand on his manhood.

A constriction formed in Fargo's throat. He had to will himself not to explode as she rubbed up and down in languid motion. Her hair fell over his face. Moving it aside, he pressed his mouth to hers. She practically devoured him.

Her hips ground light and easy to heighten their pleasure. When he cupped her bottom and dug his nails into her backside, she gasped and rubbed her nether mound harder on his pole.

Fargo hiked at her dress. It took some doing. She had to rise up for him to pull it up around her waist. Once he did, he ran his hand down one inner thigh and up the other. Her skin rippled to his touch.

Covering Delicia's bush with his palm, Fargo ran a finger

along her moist slit. She shivered deliciously. He parted her lips and moved his fingertip in small circles over her tiny knob and she raised her face to the sky and opened her mouth wide but didn't utter a sound.

Fargo lost all sense of time. There was her body, and his, and their rising need. When he finally entered her, Delicia clung to him and whispered his name. When he thrust, ever harder, her eyes grew wide and her mouth parted and she moaned deep in her throat. When he gripped her hips and imitated a steam engine piston, she matched him, stroke for stroke.

It was Delicia who gushed first. For a brief moment she was completely still, then she went into a frenzy of release, her pelvis churning, her breasts heaving. She rammed against him so hard, it was a wonder she didn't break him in half. She came and she came, and when she was spent, when she lay weak and panting, it was his turn. He rammed into her with renewed vigor until he, too, exploded with a violence that lifted both of them off the ground.

Afterward, Delicia lay with her cheek on his shoulder, her fingers stroking his hair, her eyes closed and her beautiful face composed in the contentment of sweet release.

"That was nice," she said dreamily.

"Could have been better," Fargo teased, and earned a light smack on the arm.

"I will miss you when you go," Delicia said.

"Don't."

"I'm sorry, but I will. Any woman would not mind having you for her own."

"I'm not ready to be tied down, and I never gave you the idea I was."

"I know, but I am starting to have feelings for you. Strong feelings."

"I don't want you shedding tears on my account," Fargo warned her.

"I can't help myself," Delicia said. "I'm a woman."

Fargo was uncomfortable talking about it and glad when she fell silent. He closed his eyes and let himself drift and he was almost asleep when a whinny from the Ovaro snapped him awake. He raised his head.

"What is it?" Delicia dreamily asked.

Fargo wasn't sure. The stallion was staring off into the woods with its ear pricked. Something was out there, but it could be anything—a wolf, a bobcat, a bear. Or the mysterious Hound. "Let me up."

Delicia raised her head. "Is there danger?"

Sliding out from under her, Fargo put himself together. He strapped on his gun belt, picked up the Henry, and stood. "Stay here."

He moved to the west edge of the clearing. Shadows dappled the greenery. Somewhere a squirrel was chattering. A pair of hummingbirds flitted about, and in the distance he heard the rat-a-tat of a woodpecker. All perfectly normal, but the Ovaro never whinnied without cause.

Fargo stood there until Delicia impatiently called his name. He was turning to go back to her when a shadow low to the ground did something shadows shouldn't do—it moved. Jerking the Henry to his shoulder, he took a bead. Whatever it was, it slipped behind a thicket. He waited for it to reappear and was so intent on catching sight of it that he nearly jumped when a hand fell on his shoulder.

"What's out there?" Delicia whispered.

"I don't know yet."

"I'll get the horses," she offered.

Fargo covered the thicket. If it was the Hound, he might have time for only one shot before it reached them and he must make that shot count. He continued to cover it as he climbed on the Ovaro and as he rode toward it with Delicia behind him.

"Be careful, Skye."

Fargo reined to the right to go around. He supposed he shouldn't be surprised that nothing was there. "Keep an eye out," he said, and dismounted. A few bent blades of grass were all he found.

"It could have been anything," Delicia said when he told her.

Fargo climbed back on. "I suppose."

"Something tells me that when the time comes, the beast will not be easy to kill," Delicia remarked.

Something told Fargo she was right.

24

It delighted Delicia that there had not been any new attacks on the sheep. They were grazing or resting, oblivious to their peril.

"You'll think this is silly," she said as they sat their horses and gazed out over the valley. "But I'm as attached to them as I would be to my own children."

"Wait until you have some," Fargo said.

"Sheep are in our blood," Delicia said. "My grandmother likes to say that God put sheep on this earth to teach us to be humble."

That made no sense to Fargo but all he said was, "Constanza is a fine one to talk. She's as bloodthirsty as an Apache."

"Not where sheep are concerned. She'd no more harm one than she would a baby."

Fargo had something more important on his mind. "How much of this valley have your people explored?"

Delicia shrugged. "I don't know. Some of the men have hunted in the mountains a lot. Why?"

"The Hound has to have a place to lie up."

"Find the lair and we can put an end to the monster?" Delicia nodded. "My people had the same idea. My brother and several others spent days searching but didn't find it." She looked at him. "You think it will strike again soon, don't you?"

"Odds are," Fargo said.

"I saw how upset that cowboy was when he told us about the dead cows. I believe you, now, that they are not to blame. It must be a wolf. A *lobo*."

Fargo was scanning the heights. "I have most of the afternoon to myself," he said. "I reckon I'll spend it keeping my promise to your grandpa."

"By your lonesome?" Delicia shook her head. "I'll go with you."

"No," Fargo said. He leaned over and kissed her on the cheek. "I can't hunt and protect you, both. Go back to the wagons where you'll be safe."

"What if I refuse?"

"I'll tie you over your saddle and send you back anyway."

"I believe you would," Delicia said, annoyed. But she clucked to her horse and started down.

Fargo didn't budge until he was sure she wasn't going to try to trick him and circle back.

Above the bench grew thick timber. Above the timber were difficult grades with sparse vegetation. Given the size of the valley, searching for tracks was akin to looking for the proverbial needle in a haystack.

Not that Fargo didn't find any. There were plenty of deer tracks. There were elk. He found bear sign, including a tree covered with claw and rub marks. At the highest elevations there was evidence of bighorn sheep.

Smaller game was everywhere. He came across raccoon tracks and skunk tracks, badger and weasel. A careless bobcat had left a few, and he even found a mountain lion print. He discovered coyote tracks and a few fox tracks.

But nowhere did he come across the tracks of the creature he sought.

By four in the afternoon Fargo was ready to head down. He had a long ride to the cowboy camp. He idly scanned the valley from end to end—and stiffened. On the far side, almost directly across from him, an animal was loping down an open slope. At that distance he couldn't tell much other than it had the build of a dog or a wolf but it was a lot bigger. It disappeared into a patch of pines, and although he waited another quarter of a hour, he didn't see it again.

Fargo gigged the stallion down the mountain. He reached the bench and started across. He wasn't expecting trouble. When three riders loomed at the crest he suspected they had been there all along, waiting for him.

"Hold up, gringo," Carlos demanded. "We want a word with you."

Fargo drew rein. "You don't want to do this," he said.

"But we do," Carlos said with a smirk. "Permit me to introduce my friends. On my left is Pablo, on my right is Horaz."

The other two were young, like Carlos, and like him, they were smirking at how clever they thought they were being.

"Can you guess what we want to talk about, gringo?" Carlos asked.

"You want advice on how not to be so stupid?"

Carlos lost his smirk. "Insulting me, gringo, proves that you are the one who isn't very smart."

"You won't like what happens if you do this," Fargo said.

"Can you read my thoughts now?" Carlos said. "Do you know what I am going to do before I do it?" He uttered a cold bark. "I think not."

"Have it your way," Fargo said. "We'll play this out. Go ahead and say what's on your mind."

"My sister," Carlos said.

"A fine filly," Fargo said.

"Too fine for the likes of you. You are an outsider. We do not like it when outsiders trifle with our women. I want you to stop talking to her. I want you to stop going for rides with her."

"That's up to her."

"No, it isn't. She only thinks it is." Carlos paused. "But she is just part of the reason I have come to see you. The other part is this." He touched his swollen face. "You beat me, made me look the fool."

"You had it coming."

"Who are you to judge? I was doing what I thought best to protect my people."

"And you got Alejandro killed."

"He went with me willingly. He knew what might happen."

"Is that what you tell yourself?"

"He is gone. It is pointless to talk about him. But my sister is very much alive, and I tell you now, to your face, that you have no right to be with her."

"Is that all?" Fargo wanted to be on his way.

"There is just this. Pablo, Horaz and I have had enough of you, and we are escorting you out of the valley, here and now."

"What about Trask?" Fargo said. "I'm to meet with him

tonight. You don't care that I might be able to smooth things over so that your people and the cowboys can get along?"

"Filthy gringos," Carlos said. "What gives you the idea we *want* to get along? This is our valley. They are the ones who must leave. So long as they stay, we will go on spilling their blood."

"This isn't about the good of your people," Fargo said. "It's about your hate."

Carlos put both hands on his rifle. "What will it be? Will you leave or will you die?"

25

The other two didn't have rifles or revolvers. They had knives in sheaths at their hips, and when Carlos gripped his rifle, each gripped the hilt of his weapon.

"I take back what I said about you being stupid," Fargo said.

Carlos blinked in surprise. "You do?"

"To be stupid you have to have a brain." And with that, Fargo whipped out his Colt and jabbed his spurs. The Ovaro bounded between Carlos' horse and Pablo's. With a lightning swing to either side, Fargo slammed the Colt against their heads. Carlos fell but Pablo stayed on and reined aside, reeling.

Fargo shifted to cover Horaz but Horaz did an incredible thing: He rose onto his saddle, leaped onto Carlos' horse, and from there sprang at Fargo. And as Horaz sprang, he drew his knife.

Fargo barely got his arm up in time. Horaz was big, and his weight was enough to knock him from the saddle. Each got a grip on the other's arm as they toppled. Fargo tried to turn so that Horaz bore the impact but they both came down hard on their sides. Horaz made it to his feet first. Fargo was only to his knees when the sheepherder slashed at his neck. Fargo ducked and smashed the Colt against Horaz's knee, and Horaz cried out and staggered. Fargo smashed his other knee. Horaz swore and came down on his hands and toes.

"Damn you, gringo!"

Fargo hit him once, and then again, and Horaz crumpled, unconscious.

Hooves drummed as Fargo pushed to his feet. Pablo had recovered enough to try to ride him down. Fargo darted aside and the horse swept past. Instantly, Pablo reined around to try again.

Fargo took a long bound and leaped. With his left hand he grabbed Pablo's serape even as with his right he rammed the Colt into Pablo's side. Pablo cried out, and the next moment Fargo hauled him from the saddle and slammed him to earth. Pablo groaned and went limp.

Fargo thought that was the end of it but a blow to his shoulder spun him half around. His gun arm went numb.

Carlos had his rifle by the barrel and was wielding it like a club. His face contorted in hate, he hissed, "I will cave your head in, gringo!"

Fargo dodged a swing but lost his hat. He skipped back and Carlos came after him, swearing furiously. Fargo tried to raise the Colt but his arm wouldn't work. He went to border shift, and tripped over Pablo.

Before Fargo knew it, he was flat on the ground with Carlos rearing over him and the rifle hoisted high to bash his brains out.

"Now, gringo! Now!" Carlos screamed.

Fargo rolled and the stock thudded into the dirt. Scrambling onto his knees, Fargo crossed his left hand to his right boot to try to draw the Arkansas toothpick. But Carlos came at him again, swinging. It was all he could do to twist away. His right arm was tingling but he still couldn't bring the Colt to bear.

And Pablo was slowly getting up.

Carlos swung the rifle low, seeking to sweep Fargo's legs out from under him. Leaping into the air, Fargo kicked Carlos in the chest. Gripping the Colt by the barrel with his left hand, Fargo whipped it out and around and had the satisfaction of seeing Carlo's mouth explode with blood and bits of teeth.

Carlos screeched and dropped the rifle and clutched at his face.

Fargo hit him again. There was a *crack* and Carlos dropped where he stood.

Pablo was almost to his feet. He had a hand to his head and was shaking it to clear it.

"Had enough?" Fargo said.

Pablo spun. Glaring, he clawed at the knife on his hip.

Fargo kicked him in the groin. The tip of his boot caught

the young sheepherder where it would hurt any man the most and Pablo shrieked and folded as Carlos had done. Pablo's eyelids fluttered and his body convulsed before he lay still.

Fargo looked at the three of them.

"Jackasses."

He tried his right arm and although it was tingling to where it hurt, he could move it. He proceeded to climb on the Ovaro and gathered up their horses. "Enjoy the walk," he said to the limp figures, and headed down the mountain.

The camp was quiet when he arrived. Most of the women were in their wagons; most of the men were off tending the sheep.

A few children scampered about but paid him no mind. He had tied the horses and was pouring himself a cup of coffee when Constanza stalked over, her flinty face pinched with wrath.

"Where are my grandson and his friends?"

"Here we go again."

"Don't treat me like fool," Constanza said. "I saw you ride up with their horses and I know they went to have a talk with you."

"Talk?" Fargo sipped and peered at her over the tin cup. "Your grandson tried to bash my brains out. And I bet it was with your blessing."

Constanza smiled.

Insight dawned, and Fargo said, "It was your idea, wasn't it? That grandson of yours wouldn't do anything without your say-so. Was it you who told him to kill those cows, too?"

"My grandson stands up for us, which is more than I can say about my husband." Constanza folded her arms. "Now where is he? Have you killed them?"

"I should have," Fargo said.

"You are a tough hombre, senor," Constanza said. "I will grant you that much."

"I don't give a damn what you think."

"Good. Then you won't mind my telling you that I hate you and your kind."

"Kind?" Fargo said.

"Anglos. All Anglos."

"You're one of those." Fargo had a special dislike for bigots.

He'd seen too many of them in his travels—whites who hated red men, red men who wanted all whites dead, whites who loathed blacks, blacks who despised whites, whites who looked down their noses at those they called greasers . . . and on and on it went.

"*Si*, senor," Constanza was crowing, "and proud of it. You would never understand."

"What's your excuse for hating so much?"

"Who needs one?" Constanza said. "But if you must know, I am a pureblood Spaniard, as were my father and mother and their parents and all those before them. Can you say as much?" She didn't give him a chance to respond. "Of course not, because you do not have a heritage like mine. You are nothing, and less than nothing. You are a mongrel."

"I'd rather be a mongrel than a bitch."

In indignation Constanza drew herself up to her full height. "You make it easy for me to hate you, senor."

"Don't expect me to lose sleep over it."

"It is a mistake to take me lightly," Constanza said. "I give you this warning. Forget your promise to my silly husband. We will kill the Hound ourselves. Forget about Trask and his cowboys. Climb on your horse and ride away or you will not live to see out the week."

"Your grandson made the same threat. I didn't listen to him and I'm sure as hell not going to listen to you."

"Before this is over you will wish you had," Constanza said.

26

The first thing Fargo noticed were all the new cows, more than a thousand head, with punchers riding herd.

The second thing were all the new hands. By his reckoning there were thirty or more.

There was a cook wagon, too, and a wagon for supplies. They were parked close to the trees.

The sun was about to relinquish its reign when Fargo drew rein and climbed down. He wasn't expecting a warm welcome but he wasn't expecting to be ignored, either. Yet except for a few cold stares, he was treated as if he wasn't there. "Ben Trask invited me," he said.

No one responded.

A sense of uneasiness came over him, a feeling that he was about to step into a bear trap. But he didn't fork leather and leave. He never was one for showing yellow. Hooking his thumbs in his gun belt, he sauntered to the fire and nodded at Shorty.

"I didn't reckon you would," Shorty said.

"You said your boss wanted to see me."

Griff Wexler came over from the cook wagon. "It's the only reason you're still breathin', mister."

Another man was behind the foreman. Not much taller than Shorty, he was almost as wide as he was tall. His shoulders and chest were broad and powerful, his arms uncommonly long. On his right hip was a Smith and Wesson. "Behave yourself, Griff," he said sternly.

"Trask, I take it?" Fargo said.

"Ben Trask," Trask amended, and held out his hand.

It was the strongest handshake Fargo ever felt. For a second he thought that Trask was trying to break his fingers but the rancher's grip eased and Trask smiled and motioned. "Have a seat. I promised you a feed and I always keep my word." He waited for Fargo to sit and then sank facing him, his legs crossed, his forearms on his knees. "Hope you don't mind beef and potatoes."

"I've never met a cow I didn't want to eat," Fargo said.

"Cows or whores?" Trask said, and burst into gruff mirth. He glanced at a cowboy and snapped his fingers, and just-like-that a tin cup brimming with coffee was placed in his hands. "One for our guest, too."

Fargo decided he would let his host bring up why he'd been invited. For now he was content to take the man's measure.

"Skye Fargo," Trask said. "I've heard of you. Hell, most anyone who can read has heard of you."

"Hell," Fargo said.

"That's what you get for bein' half famous."

"It wasn't by choice."

"No," Trask said. "I can tell just by lookin' at you that you're not one of those fancy pants who puts on airs and pretends to be somethin' he ain't. You're the real article, sure enough."

"I like to think I am," Fargo said, for lack of anything better.

"I like to think I am, too," Trask said. "So tell me. You ever hear of me before you met some of my boys the other day?"

"Can't say as I have, no," Fargo admitted.

Trask chuckled. "Hear that, boys? Here I think I'm the cock of the walk in west Texas, and a famous feller like Fargo, here, doesn't know me from Adam."

"I don't know many ranchers," Fargo said.

"No need to spare my feelin's. My hide's inches thick." Trask drained half his cup. "I reckon the place to start is to set you straight about me."

"It's the sheepherders I'm here about," Fargo began.

Trask held up a calloused hand. "We'll get to them directly. Just listen a spell." He rubbed his square chin. "I run the Bar T, one of the biggest outfits in this part of the country, or most anywhere else, for that matter. It has more acres than some states, and we're always addin' on."

"How big, exactly?" Fargo asked.

"Eh?" Ben Task gestured. "Last I checked, it was six hundred thousand acres, give or take forty or fifty thousand.

I run about seventy-five thousand head. Got some hogs and goats too, but they don't hardly count."

"Seventy-five thousand?" Fargo repeated in some astonishment.

"That's a heap of cows," Trask agreed, "which is why I'm always on the lookout for new land to graze."

"Uh-oh," Fargo said.

"We ain't to it yet but we will be soon." Trask nodded at Griff Wexler. "My foreman says he told you that I heard about this valley from some boys of mine who moseyed up this way to hunt elk. He says he made it plain as plain can be that I aim to lay claim to it."

"He did," Fargo said.

Trask grunted. "Then I don't know quite what to make of you. You don't *look* stupid."

"How's that again?"

"I have pretty near forty hands with me. Any time I want, I can send a rider for forty more."

"Your own little army," Fargo said.

"That's a good way of puttin' it, only it's not so little. And every hombre on my spread, from my bronc breakers to my line riders to my brush poppers, they're all loyal to the brand." Trask glanced at Shorty. "Ain't that right?"

"It sure as hell is, boss," Shorty declared, and a number of the punchers nodded or voiced agreement.

"I didn't get where I am by bein' puny," Trask said. "I take what I want when I want it."

"Even if somebody was there before you?" Fargo asked.

Trask scowled. "Mister, it's not my fault if these sheepherders never thought to file a legal claim. I always file on land I make my own."

Fargo could see where this was going and didn't like it.

"But to back up a bit, my foreman told you about the Bar T and about me and how Hermanos Valley will be called Trask Valley before too long, did he not?"

"Except for the Trask Valley part," Fargo said.

"Then I'll say it again," Trask said. "I don't know what to make of you, because only a fool would do what you've done."

"Refresh my memory," Fargo said.

Trask leaned toward him. Trask's face was steel and fire. "You've made me mad, mister. Do you know what happens to people who make me mad?" His hand darted down and when he raised it he had a beetle between his thick thumb and forefinger. The beetle struggled, its legs kicking. "I'll give you a hint," he said, and crushed the beetle to a pulp.

27

Ben Trask wiped his fingers on his pants and smiled. There was no warmth in his smile, no friendliness. "We'll eat and then we'll get to it."

Fargo didn't ask what "it" was.

Trask snapped his fingers again and a cowhand brought a plate heaped with a thick slab of steak and potatoes.

Another puncher brought a plate for Fargo.

Trask poked at his meat with a fork and said, "This came from one of the cows killed by . . . what the hell is it? I thought maybe the sheepherders had sicced a dog on my herd but my boys say the mutton lovers have lost sheep, too."

"They've lost a lot more sheep than you've lost cows," Fargo said.

"What's killin' everything?"

"I've seen its tracks and I've caught sight of it twice and I still don't know what it is."

"How can that be?" Trask said. "From what I've heard, you're supposed to be one of the best scouts breathin'."

"I've hunted most everything at one time or another," Fargo said, "but this thing has me stumped." He cut off a piece of juicy beef. "I agreed to hunt it for them but so far it has me licked."

"Why would you do a thing like that? Help them, I mean? What are they to you?"

"Nothing special."

"Then why, damn it? Help me to understand."

"It killed a little girl."

"Oh," Trask said, and then again, more thoughtfully. "Oh. I didn't know."

"It's killed two of their men, besides."

"I don't much care about the grownups," Trask said. "If they raise sheep, they're maggots. But kids now, that's different.

I have two daughters. This changes things." He lapsed into a silence that he didn't break until both of them had cleaned their plates and were washing the meal down with more coffee. Out of the blue he said, "That little girl has saved your bacon. For now."

"She has?"

Trask nodded. "Three of my punchers are dead. Two of them, I understand, were shot by you."

"They were trying to kill me."

"Doesn't matter. No one kills a Bar T hand and lives. No one." Trask stared at him. "I invited you over to get a look at you and try to figure what makes you tick, and then I was fixin' to have my boys beat you and strip you and drag you behind a horse until the skin was flayed from your body."

"It wouldn't be easy."

"Easy or hard, once I make up my mind, it gets done." Trask paused. "I make my own laws, Fargo, and the top law is that the Bar T and those who work for me come before all else. I'm fair about it. I don't go hangin' rustlers without I have proof they've rustled. I catch a brand blotter workin' on my critters, I don't always kill them. Sometimes I chop off their hands as a message to others with the same notion."

"You call that fair?"

Trask nodded. "In this country a man can't afford to be puny. Not if he's to make somethin' of himself. I have to be tough to keep what I have."

"They were trying to kill me," Fargo said again. "They didn't leave me any choice."

"I believe you. And I'll take that into account. But you shouldn't have come down here with those two woolly lovers."

"I didn't. I came to try and stop them."

"Well now," Trask said, and his thick eyebrows met over his nose. "Why are you explainin' yourself? You don't strike me as the type."

"I don't want to have to kill any more of your men," Fargo said. "But if they make me, I will. And I won't stop with them. I'll go straight to the top."

Ben Trask sat up. His features shifted, first in surprise, then anger, and then he let loose with a belly laugh. "Did you hear him, boys?"

"We sure enough did, boss," Shorty said. "Say the word and we'll bed him down, permanent."

"Like hell you will," Trask said, grinning. "Don't you see what we've got here?"

Shorty and some of the others exchanged confused looks.

It was Griff Wexler who said, "I'm afraid we've lost your trail, Mr. Trask."

"What we've got here," the rancher said, "is a man."

"We're all men, boss," Shorty said.

Trask looked at him. "You're young yet or you'd know there are men and then there are *men*." He switched his gaze to Fargo and nodded in approval. "Him and me are of the same breed."

Fargo didn't see it that way but he was sensible enough not to say so.

"Yes, sir," Trask continued. "This puts everythin' in a whole new light."

"It does?" Griff said.

Fargo took advantage of his host's newfound friendliness to say, "I don't suppose you'd be willing to share Hermanos Valley with the sheepherders?"

"Not on your life," Trask said. "Sheep destroy the range for cattle. It's either them or us who stays and it won't be them."

So much for friendliness, Fargo reflected. "They won't go without a fight."

"That's up to them."

"There are women and children."

Trask frowned. "I told you I'm fair. I don't make war on females and kids. But I don't let them turn me to mush, neither."

Fargo didn't know what else to say. He had tried every argument.

Just then a fierce howl was wafted down the valley by the night wind. The cry rose to a savage pitch that caused some of the horses to whinny and stomp.

"God Almighty," Trask exclaimed. "Was that it?"

Fargo nodded.

"I've never heard the like." Trask stared into the darkness. "It wasn't a wolf. And it didn't sound like no dog. But what else could it be?"

Fargo had no answer.

"All right," Trask said. "Here's how it will be. For the time bein' I'll hold off on the woolly lovers. You can tell them for me that we have a truce."

"Boss?" Shorty said.

Trask gestured sharply. "A truce," he repeated. "We'll stay at this end of the valley and they stay at the other end. But only until we find that thing and end its cow-killin' days."

"And little girl killing days," Fargo said.

"We're goin' to hunt it?" Griff said.

"We'll start tomorrow. Every last hand except for those ridin' herd will lend a hand."

"That's generous of you," Fargo said.

Trask laughed. "Don't be thankin' me. I'm only doin' it so you can kill the thing and be on your way. I'm startin' to like you, and I'd hate to have to bury you."

"I'd hate to have to be buried," Fargo said.

28

The sheepherders greeted the news of a truce with elation,

Porfiro was the happiest of all. "I prayed he would see reason and he has. This is wonderful."

Constanza muttered in exasperation and then snapped, "Haven't you heard a word the scout has said? The rancher still intends to drive us out."

"We have bought time," Porfiro said. "We can persuade him to live in peace."

"There are days when I wonder why I married you," Constanza said bitterly. "As soon as the Hound is dead, this Trask will turn his guns on us."

For once Fargo agreed with her. But for now he was willing to concentrate on the beast. "Trask and his men will be here early," he informed them. "We plan to split into groups of four or five and search the valley from end to end."

"Do you really think you can bring the Hound to bay?" Delicia asked.

Fargo shrugged. The valley itself encompassed some sixty square miles. Then there were the adjacent slopes. Even with fifty or more searchers, finding the beast would be more luck than anything. He went to lead the Ovaro around to the horse string but Constanza grabbed his arm.

"Hold on. I demand to know where my grandson is."

"What?" Fargo said in genuine surprise.

"You told me he would show up but he hasn't. Where did you leave him?"

"Up on that tableland where you graze half your sheep," Fargo said. "They should have been here hours ago."

"Perhaps they decided to remain overnight," Porfiro said, "to keep watch."

"No." Constanza shook her head. "I told him not to stay out with the Hound on the loose."

"He is young and always thinks he knows best," Porfiro said.

"He would listen to me," Constanza insisted. "That boy worships the ground I walk on."

Must be nice, Fargo almost said. Instead, he gripped the saddle horn and swung back onto the Ovaro. "I'll go have a look."

"You won't be back until after midnight," Porfiro said, "and we must get an early start tomorrow."

"Don't you care about your grandson?" Constanza demanded. "If the gringo wants to go, let him."

"What good can he do in the dark?" Porfiro argued.

The matter was decided by a savage bray from out of the woods to the east of the camp. The horses did as the Bar T animals had done, and acted up.

"The Hound is after our mounts!" a sheepherder cried.

Fargo gigged the Ovaro. While the men calmed their animals, he rode back and forth between the trees and the string. He yearned for a shot, just one clear shot, but the creature was too clever to show itself.

The string quieted, and in a while Fargo drew rein. He was sitting there when Delicia's hand found his boot.

"A word, if you please," she said quietly.

Fargo didn't take his eyes off the benighted vegetation. "I'm listening."

"Carlos is my brother and I care for him even though he can be obnoxious at times."

"And?" Fargo prompted when she stopped.

"I care for you, too. Stay the night and go look for him in the morning. It is too dangerous to go off by yourself."

Fargo had no real hankering to go. He felt he should only because he'd taken their horses. And in the dark he couldn't do much other than shout their names. As he was debating, two men with rifles were posted to stand guard and Porfiro ushered the rest of his people back to the fires.

"You haven't answered me," Delicia said.

Fargo swung down to talk it over—and Constanza was in front of him.

"What do you think you are doing? Climb back on and go find my grandson."

"I have convinced him to do it in the morning, Grandmother," Delicia said.

"Now." Constanza poked Fargo in the chest. "I warn you. If he comes to harm because of you, I will kill you myself."

"Abuela!" Delicia exclaimed.

"I will," Constanza said, and stormed off.

"I'm sorry," Delicia said. "She has never been shy in expressing her sentiments. But I do not think she would really kill you."

Fargo wasn't so certain. He stripped the stallion and carried his saddle and bedroll to the wagon, slid them under, and bent to slide under himself.

"Turning in so early?" Delicia asked.

"It's been a long day," Fargo said. And he'd gotten little sleep the night before.

"I was thinking you and I might go for a walk."

Fargo couldn't believe he was about to say what he was about to say. "Not tonight."

Her disappointment as plain as her lovely nose, Delicia pouted and said, "I guess you're right. My grandmother is mad enough as it is." She turned away and glanced over her shoulder. "But there is always tomorrow night."

Undoing his bedroll, Fargo spread his blankets, propped his saddle behind him, and laid back. All that he had been through, and he hadn't accomplished much. The cowboys and the sheepherders were still at odds. Then there was the Hound or whatever it was, still out there, killing to its heart's content.

Fargo closed his eyes and pulled his hat brim down. He should be grateful for the truce, he supposed, but it was only temporary. Once the Hound was dead, all hell was liable to break loose.

As if to taunt him, an eerie howl pierced the night to the south. The creature was paying the Texans and their cows a visit.

Fargo marveled at how swiftly it had gotten from the north end of the valley to the south end. He hoped the cowboys got a shot at it. He didn't care who killed it, just so it was dead.

He thought about the dogs the thing had killed, and how the hunch he had might not be so crazy, after all. Before he could ponder further, he was sucked into the void of sleep.

29

The cowboys came up the valley riding two abreast with Ben Trask and Griff Wexler at their head. The morning sun glinted off their cartridges and belt buckles and hardware. From a distance they could pass for an army patrol.

"Hay tantos," Porfiro said. "There are so many."

"We can't trust them, Grandfather," Carlos said.

The hothead and his friends had turned up in the middle of the night. It took them so long to get back because Carlos had sprained his ankle and couldn't bear to put weight on it. He'd cut a tree limb for a crutch and was using it now.

"You will behave," Porfiro said. "I will only warn you once."

The sheepherders had been talking excitedly but they fell silent and fidgeted and cast anxious glances at one another as the Texans approached.

"How do we know they will not exterminate us where we stand?" Constanza said.

"Trask gave his word," Fargo said.

Constanza mimicked spitting on the ground. "The word of a gringo. What is it worth?"

"A man like Trask," Fargo replied, "his word is everything."

"I don't trust any of you Anglos as far as I can throw you."

"I'm shocked," Fargo said.

The rancher brought his men to a stop. "Folks," he said simply, and stayed on his horse.

Porfiro walked over and held out his hand. "Mr. Trask, *yo soy, el líder aquí.*"

"Say that in white talk," Trask said gruffly.

"I am the leader here. On behalf of my people, I welcome you and your vaqueros, and thank you for your help."

"We're not here for your benefit," Trask said. "We're here because I don't like losin' cows to man nor beast."

"Still, you came. Why not climb down? We have made extra coffee and have food."

"I wouldn't eat sheep if I was starvin'," Trask said. "Mutton is the worst meat there is."

"Have you ever had any, senor?" Porfiro asked.

"Hell no."

"We have other food besides meat. There are frijoles. Tortillas. And more. All of it good, I promise you."

"No is no," Trask said.

"Very well," Porfiro said. "Then at least let us welcome you in traditional fashion." He clapped his hands and half a dozen children stepped forward. Four were girls, holding flowers.

Yoana stepped up and held her flowers aloft. "For you, senor."

"It won't work," Trask said to Porfiro.

"Senor?"

"Usin' your kids to get at me." Trask motioned at Yoana. "I don't want the damn flowers, girl."

"It is to thank you, senor," Yoana said, "for helping to hunt the animal that killed my friend, Angelita."

Trask glowered at Fargo. "Was this your idea? Tell them they're wastin' their breath. I'll do what I have to when the time comes."

"I had no part in it," Fargo said.

"That is true, Senor Trask," Porfiro said. "Please. Yoana and the others will be most upset if you do not accept their gifts."

Trask started to swear and caught himself. His jaw muscles twitching, he bent down. "Hand 'em over girl. But it doesn't make us friends."

"Would you like to see Angelita's grave?" Yoana asked.

"Why should I bother? She's nothin' to me."

"She was my best friend, senor," Yoana said sadly. "The Hound tore her throat out."

"Damn you for this," Trask said to Porfiro.

"Senor?"

Trask looked at the flowers in his hand. He made as if to cast them down, then glanced at Yoana. Reaching behind him, he opened a saddlebag, carefully placed the flowers inside, and closed it. "We'll get the thing that did it, girl. Your friend can rest easy."

"I would rather Angelita was alive, senor," Yoana said. "We had such good times. She made me laugh a lot."

"My own girls made me smile when they were little," Trask said. "They're pretty near full grown now."

"And they don't make you smile anymore?" Yoana asked.

Trask's throat bobbed and he nodded, once. "Yes, girl, they do." Suddenly straightening, he barked at Porfiro, "Enough jawin'. Let's get this hunt started."

Fargo climbed on the Ovaro and reined it next to the rancher. "You handled that well."

"I should shoot the son of a bitch."

"He didn't do it to win you over."

"The hell he didn't," Trask said. "And we're done talkin' about it."

"Why don't you leave Mr. Trask be?" Griff Wexler said.

"Say the word, Mr. Trask," Shorty said. "We'll show these sheep lovers how we feel about 'em."

"No one lifts a finger unless I say so," Trask commanded.

"Of course, boss," Griff said.

Trask turned to Fargo. "You've hunted this animal. You've seen it, you said. Where do you suggest we start lookin'?"

"It could be anywhere," Fargo said. "We only hear it at night so at first I thought it lays up during the day. But then it killed those sheep and cows in broad daylight."

"Wolves like high up," Trask mentioned. "They dig dens ten, fifteen feet long. Even I know that much."

"It's not a wolf."

"So you keep sayin'. But that wasn't no dog we heard. So I ask you again. What the hell is it?"

"If I knew that," Fargo said, "I'd be a happy man." He remembered his last thoughts before he fell asleep, and he mentioned, "The first thing it did was kill their dogs."

"What was that?" Trask said.

"It killed their dogs before it went after their sheep and your cows."

"All the dogs at once?"

"I didn't think to ask." Fargo looked over at where Porfiro was climbing onto his horse and called his name. "Those dogs of yours?"

"Senor?"

"Did the Hound kill all of them on the same night?"

"Oh, no, senor. It was over the course of a week or so. One at a time."

"Damn," Trask said.

"How's that matter?" Griff Wexler asked.

"It's important as hell," Trask said.

Skye Fargo agreed.

30

They split into a dozen groups and fanned out in all directions.

Fargo was with four men: Carlos, Shorty and two other cowboys, Billy-Bob and Hank. Trask had told Shorty and the other two to go with him, and then Porfiro came over and asked if he'd be willing to keep an eye on Carlos.

So here they were. It was the middle of the morning and they were high on a mountain to the east of the valley. He called a halt in a meadow to rest their horses. As they climbed down, Carlos started in.

"So tell me gringo," he said to Shorty, "what gives you the right to lord it over us?"

"Watch that mouth of yours, boy," Shorty said, "or me and my pards will close it."

The young puncher called Billy-Bob chuckled. "Looks to me as if someone has already pounded on him somethin' awful."

"That was me," Fargo said. "And none of you are laying a hand on anyone else."

"Says you," Shorty said. "The boss told us to ride with you. He didn't say take your orders."

"Then we might as well get it settled." Fargo didn't like to show off but he had to put them in their place now or it would only get worse. He faced the three cowboys. "Whenever you're ready, draw."

"Say again?" Hank said.

"Fill your hands," Fargo said.

Shorty chuckled. "Are you loco? You want us to throw down on you?"

"If you can."

"Listen to him," Billy-Bob said. "Mister, I should warn you. I'm one of the fastest on the Bar T. I don't mean to brag but it's a fact."

"Shot a lot of men, have you?"

"Well, no," Billy-Bob said. "Not any, actually. But I'm still fast as hell."

"He's greased lightnin'," Shorty said.

"Then you'll do," Fargo said. "Go for that hogleg any time you want."

"You *are* loco," Billy-Bob said, and his hand stabbed for his revolver.

Fargo had his Colt out and the hammer back before the cowboy began to draw.

Billy-Bob froze. "Jesus God Almighty."

"Whoo-eee," Hank blurted in awe. "I didn't see his hand move."

"It don't mean nothin'," Shorty said.

Fargo let down the hammer. He twirled the Colt forward and twirled it backward and did a flip and caught it and smoothly twirled it into his holster. "I don't want any trouble from anyone." He stared at Carlos. "That includes you."

"I will do as I please, gringo."

"Your face isn't swollen enough?"

Carlos' eyes became slits of hate. Wheeling on his heel, he stalked off.

The cowboys were staring at Fargo's Colt.

"Where'd you learn to handle a six-shooter like that?" Hank asked.

"Practice," Fargo said. Many an evening on the trail, he'd amuse himself with pistol tricks and practicing his draw to where it became as natural as breathing.

"You could have gunned me without half tryin'," Billy-Bob said.

"Worth keeping in mind," Fargo noted.

"You're awful uppity," Shorty said. "And don't think I've forgot you killed two of our own."

"I've been all through that with your boss."

"Mr. Trask may say that you had cause but I ain't one to turn the other cheek."

Shorty hitched at his gun belt and walked away.

"Better watch yourself, mister," Hank said. "He was real close to Lathrop, one of those fellers you shot."

"What about you two?"

Hank shrugged. "I do as Mr. Trask says, and Mr. Trask says we're to leave you be."

Billy-Bob pushed his hat back on his head. "Mr. Trask said it was a mix-up, that you were tryin' to help out. That's good enough for me."

Fargo was relieved that he wouldn't have to keep an eye on them, too. He had enough on his hands with Shorty and Carlos.

The former was glaring at the world. Carlos had gone into the cottonwoods and was out of sight. He went to find him.

A dozen steps into the cottonwoods a ribbon of blue sparkled. Carlos was on a knee examining bare dirt.

"I was just about to yell for you to come have a look."

There had to be twenty paw prints. Huge, well defined, they were the same as those Fargo had seen before—neither wolf nor dog nor coyote.

"Look at the size," Carlos marveled. "The thing must be as big as a bear."

"Not by half," Fargo said. "And it's not the size we have to worry about."

"I know, gringo. It's that the beast is so damn blood-thirsty."

"Worse," Fargo said.

Confused, Carlos said, "What can be worse than that?"

"There are two of them."

31

"The hell you say," Carlos said.

Squatting, Fargo touched one of the prints. "This is a right forepaw." He touched another. "This is a right forepaw, too. Notice anything?"

"They look the same to me."

"Look closer."

Carlos tilted his head one way and then the other. He held his hand to the first forepaw and then to the second. Finally he said, "One is wider than the other."

"Look at the pads."

"They are deeper on the first one than on the second." Carlos snapped his fingers. "That means one of them is heavier."

"Bigger *and* heavier," Fargo said. "It could be a male and a female."

"But a male and a female *what*?"

"That's the question," Fargo said. Standing, he followed the tracks to where the stream narrowed. The prints pointed at the water and disappeared.

Taking a few steps back to build up speed, Fargo bounded at the stream and leaped over it. He landed lightly on the balls of his feet. More tracks led into the woods.

Carlos was watching him. "Can you tell how long ago were they made?"

"This morning."

"*Suerte nos ha favorcido.* Then we have a chance of catching up to them, yes?"

"We sure as hell do." Fargo jumped back across the stream and jogged to the horses, bellowing to the cowboys, "Mount up! We found a fresh trail."

Billy-Bob and Hank came on the run, their spurs jangling. Shorty was a bit slower.

"You mean we'll get a shot at that varmint?" Billy-Bob asked.

"At both of them, maybe."

The cowboys stopped and looked at one another.

"There's two now?" Billy-Bob said.

Fargo was already climbing on. He reined around and tapped his spurs and reached the cottonwoods as Carlos burst out of them and headed for his mount. A flick of his reins, and Fargo was across the stream.

The beasts had continued east, into dense woodland. The sign was intermittent; a track here, a partial print there, a smudge farther on. It helped that the two animals made no attempt to hide their spoor, as a fox would. They were good at sticking to cover, though. They had climbed above the timber to a mostly open slope where the pair had zigzagged from boulder to boulder until they reached the top. From there they had climbed through tall grass to a stand of aspens.

Fargo recollected hearing that the Guadalupe Mountains were one of only three ranges in all of Texas where aspens could be found. He entered the stand and made a discovery that brought a smile. Flattened grass showed where the pair had rested for a while.

Once on the move the animals again traveled east.

Usually wild creatures meandered all over the place but these two were making a beeline for somewhere.

Fargo went another quarter of a mile when he abruptly drew rein and looked back. "Son of a bitch."

No one was following him.

Clucking to the Ovaro, Fargo retraced his route. When he came to the timber he cupped a hand to his mouth to shout for Carlos and the cowboys but thought better of it. The beasts might be closer than he thought, and would hear him.

His anger growing, he went lower. He had gone a quarter of a mile when he heard a mocking laugh and voices.

Fargo slowed.

"How do you like it, sheep eater?" That was Shorty's voice.

Fargo skirted a pine and stopped. The three punchers were standing and grinning at the object of their amusement.

Carlos hung by his legs from a rope that had been thrown over a tree limb and tied fast. His head was only four or five feet above the ground. He was swaying like a pendulum, and blood trickled from a corner of his mouth.

"Ready to say you are sorry, mutton man?" Shorty said.

"Go to hell, gringo, and take your amigos with you," Carlos blustered.

"An apology," Shorty said, "or you can hang up there until the chickens come home, and there ain't no chickens."

Billy-Bob laughed. "That's a good one, Shorty."

"It was your fault, not mine," Carlos said angrily. "You wanted an excuse to string me up like a criminal."

"If we'd strung you up, sheep boy, the rope would be around your neck." Shorty balled his right fist and smacked it against his left palm. "You have to learn respect for your betters." He cocked his arm. "How about I beat on you some?"

"How about you don't?" Fargo said.

Shorty whirled, his hand poised to draw. "This doesn't concern you."

"I warned you," Fargo said.

Hank put a hand on Shorty's arm. "Don't draw on him. You saw how fast he is."

"Let go," Shorty said, shaking the hand off. "So what if he's fast? I'll still put lead into him." He glanced at Billy-Bob. "How about it? You in with me?"

"The boss said not to."

"The boss ain't here. And this busybody has it comin' for killin' Lathrop and Baxter."

"Count me out," Hank said.

Billy-Bob shook his head. "Count me out, too. I'm sorry, Shorty, but I won't cross Mr. Trask."

"Fine," Shorty snapped. "Be yellow, then." He sidled to the left, his eyes glittering. "You have it to do," he said to Fargo.

"Kill him, senor!" Carlos cried.

"Shut up, greaser," Shorty growled, not taking his gaze from Fargo.

"Shorty, please," Hank said.

"It's not worth it," Billy-Bob urged.

"Weak sisters, the both of you," Shorty insulted them. His body went rigid. "How about you, scout? Nothin' to say before we get to it?"

"Die if you want to," Fargo said.

Shorty went for his six-shooter.

32

Fargo had gone out of his way to avoid trouble. But he was done avoiding. There was only so much stupid he would abide. He drew and his Colt was out and up before Shorty cleared leather. He shot Shorty in the shoulder and the cowboy spun half around but didn't go down. Cursing, Shorty did a border shift, flipping his six-gun to his other hand.

"Don't," Fargo said.

Shorty didn't listen. He raised the revolver to take better aim.

Fargo shot him again. The slug smashed into Shorty's gut, folding Shorty in half and knocking the breath out of him. Shorty staggered, dropped his smoke wagon, and clasped his hands to his belly.

"I'm hit, boys."

Fargo cocked the Colt and leveled it at Billy-Bob and Hank.

"No sir," Hank said, holding up his hands. "I want no part of this."

"Shorty shouldn't of drawn on you," Billy-Bob said. "Mr. Trask said we're not to give you trouble."

"Cut Carlos down," Fargo commanded. He eased the hammer on his Colt but kept the Colt in his hand and swung down and went over to Shorty, who had collapsed on his side.

Shorty's mouth was clenched and blood was streaming from between his fingers.

"Damn you," Fargo said.

Shorty sputtered and said, "I couldn't help it. I hate woollies. I hate those who raise them."

"Sheep aren't worth dying over," Fargo said.

Shorty coughed and groaned and said to Hank, "Tell Mr. Trask it wasn't Fargo's fault. It was me."

Hank nodded, and his throat bobbed.

Billy-Bob got Carlos down.

Casting the rope aside, Carlos came over and sneered at Shorty.

"Serves you right, gringo, for being so stupid."

"You should talk," Fargo said.

"He's a pig. All gringos are pigs. I will spit on him when he dies."

"You do," Fargo said, "and you'll be gumming your food the rest of your life."

"You don't scare me," Carlos declared.

Fargo cocked the Colt again and with a quick motion pressed the muzzle to Carlos' forehead. "Don't I?"

Carlos gulped, and glowered, and backed away. "You'd do it, too. You like to squeeze the trigger, don't you?"

"I like to shoot jackasses," Fargo said. "Which puts you at the top of the list."

"Go to hell," Carlos spat, and turning, he walked toward the horses.

"I wish you'd plugged him," Hank said.

"I still might before this is done. What brought this on?"

"Oh," Billy-Bob said. "We were followin' you and Shorty took it into his head to cut the sheepherder off. The sheepherder called him names and Shorty called him names and one thing led to another and Shorty roped him and hung him by his heels."

"Everyone forgot about the animals we're after?"

"I reckon we did," Hank said sheepishly.

"There's no shortage of idiots in this world," Fargo said in disgust.

Shorty did more coughing and gazed at the sky. "I don't want to die."

"Who does?" Fargo said.

"What was I thinkin'?"

Fargo almost said, "You weren't," but he held his anger in check. "I can try to dig the slug out."

"No need," Shorty said. "I can feel myself fadin'."

Fargo holstered his Colt. Belly wounds, as he well knew, were unpredictable. Sometimes the victim lasted for days, sometimes they went fast.

"I wonder," Shorty said, "if I'll see the pearly gates."

"Remember to be polite to any angels you meet," Hank said. "They're the ones with wings."

"Send my war bag and my poke to my brother," Shorty requested. He closed his eyes and his cheek sank to the grass. "I'm near to death, boys."

"God damn you, Shorty," Billy-Bob said.

Carlos had climbed on his horse and was smiling in sadistic delight.

"Fargo?" Shorty said.

"I'm here."

"Want to hear somethin' funny? I never shot anyone my whole life. Never had to. You're the first one I tried to buck out in gore."

"You should have picked someone slower."

Shorty grinned, and coughed, and quaked from his hat to his boots. "I never was too smart." He sucked in a deep breath, and died.

"Well now," Hank said. "He went out nice."

Fargo looked at him.

"He did," Hank said. "He didn't blubber or whine or nothin'."

"I might do me some blubberin' when I die," Billy-Bob said, "lessen I go quick."

"Let's get to the burying," Fargo directed. He found a downed branch, the punchers did the same, and working together they dug a shallow grave. Hank stripped Shorty of his valuables and gun belt and they wrapped him in a blanket and lowered the body into the hole.

"Anyone want to say anythin'?" Billy-Bob asked.

"I'm not much for quotin' Scripture," Hank said. "All I know is 'thou shalt not kill' and 'do unto others.'"

Both of them looked at Fargo.

"Do I look like a parson?" Fargo said. "But you want words? How about these." He paused. "May Shorty rest in peace. He was loyal to the brand and he loved cows."

"That's beautiful," Hank said.

"I wouldn't mind havin' that on my gravestone," Billy-Bob said.

Hank began to shove dirt in. "I reckon we should cover him so we can get after those wolves or whatever they are."

"Amen to that," Fargo said.

33

Until well into the afternoon they wound steadily deeper into the mountains. It was pushing three o'clock by Fargo's reckoning when they crested a ridge onto a broad tableland.

Forest so thick that even the bright sun of midday couldn't penetrate covered most of it.

"Spooky place," Hank said.

Fargo was more interested in gray tendrils rising into the sky half a mile away. "Look there," he said, and pointed.

"Injuns, you think?" Billy-Bob wondered.

"I doubt it," Fargo said. Few Indians would give their presence away like that.

"There ain't no white men this far out," Hank said, "unless maybe it's a hunter."

Carlos' sneer had become a fixture. "Why do you assume they are white, gringo? My people were here long before yours."

"You know of any who'd be out this way?" Hank said.

"If I did I wouldn't tell you."

Fargo shifted in his saddle. "If you do you better tell me."

Carlos glanced at the Colt in Fargo's holster. "No, senor. I am as perplexed as the rest of you."

"We should pay them a visit," Billy-Bob suggested.

"We'll stick with the tracks," Fargo said, and resumed following the sign. It was harder to do. The leaves and pine needles that covered much of the ground bore few prints. It wasn't long before he realized that the tracks were leading toward the smoke. "Well, what do you know," he said, and informed the others.

"Could be all we'll find are bodies," Billy-Bob said.

Fargo went slowly, his hand always on his revolver. In a while the forest thinned and then came to an end at the mouth of a canyon. The smoke rose from somewhere in its depths.

"Maybe it really is Injuns," Billy-Bob said. "We ain't careful, we could be pincushions."

Fargo climbed down and handed the Ovaro's reins to him. "Hold on to these."

"What are you doin'?"

"I can be quieter on foot," Fargo said. "Wait here."

"What if somethin' happens to you? How will we know?"

"You'll hear a lot of noise." Fargo yanked the Henry from the scabbard and worked the lever to feed a cartridge into the chamber.

"Take one of us or the Mex along," Hank said. "Just in case."

"I refuse to," Carlos said. "Let him do it on his own."

Fargo entered the canyon. It was several hundred feet across and green with vegetation, the sort of place that Indians would like. He came to a bend. The smell of the smoke was so strong, he almost sneezed. Crouching, he peered around. To say he was surprised was an understatement.

A crude dwelling stood near a spring. Constructed of interwoven tree limbs and sticks, it was only five feet high and about six feet wide. There was no door and no windows, only an oval opening.

Two mules were tied to a tree, both dozing in the midday heat.

Fargo didn't see their owner—or the animals he had spent most of the day tracking. Warily rising, he moved closer, the Henry pressed to his shoulder.

The mules roused and regarded him with mild interest.

Fargo smelled a foul odor and heard buzzing. Off to his right flies were swarming. He looked closer and saw bones and bits of hide, and antlers—the remains of a deer, killed not that long ago.

At the opening Fargo stopped. "Anyone home?" he called out. When he got no answer he poked his head in. The odor wasn't much better, and it was black as pitch.

Fargo drew back. He went around to the side and found a large pile of bones and fur. Poking at it with the rifle, he recognized bits and pieces of squirrel and rabbit and other game.

He walked back to the front and placed the Henry's stock on the ground and leaned on it. "Where could you have gotten to?" he wondered out loud.

"Right here, mister."

A man had come around the mules. Older than Methuselah, he had snow-white hair that fell past his shoulders and a snow-white beard that fell to his waist. His face was bronzed by exposure to the sun, and seamed with wrinkles. There was nothing friendly about his expression or the old Hawken rifle he had trained on Fargo's chest. "One wrong twitch," he warned, "and it'll be your last."

"I'm friendly," Fargo said.

"I'm not."

"I didn't come alone," Fargo thought it prudent to say.

The man's head jerked up and he scoured the surrounding woods. "These friends of yours must be invisible."

"They're out there and they'll hear if you shoot."

The old man gnawed on his lips.

"Who are you and what are you doing here?" Fargo asked.

"That's none of your damn business." The man was still scanning the trees.

"I've got my reasons for asking."

"You're not just nosy?"

"We're after two animals that have been killing cows, sheep and people."

"Oh. Them," the man said, and lowered the Hawken to his side but kept it pointed at Fargo.

"You've seen these things?" Fargo said. "You know what they are?"

"I've only ever caught a glimpse once or twice," the man said. "I hear them a lot, though, mostly at night. As to what they are, they're not wolves."

"I already know that."

"You do?" The man wagged the Hawken. "Suppose you drop that rifle before my trigger finger gets itchy."

"No," Fargo said.

"I mean it," the old man warned. "Either you do it or I shoot you."

"You're welcome to try," Fargo said.

34

Tension crackled, and for a moment Fargo thought the man would fire. Instead, he absently tugged at his beard.

"I reckon I shouldn't have come on you like I done but I don't trust strangers."

"I don't trust them much myself," Fargo said.

The old man appraised Fargo with piercing gray eyes and finally said, "My name is Rolf. Igmar Rolf. What's yours?"

Fargo told him.

"It's been a coon's age since I had visitors. I'm off the beaten path and like it that way."

"How long have you been here?" Fargo asked.

"I haven't kept track."

"Weeks? Months? Years?"

"Long enough," Rolf said. He motioned at the woods. "Call in those friends of yours so we can get acquainted."

"When I'm ready."

"You're a cautious coon, sure enough." Rolf nodded. "I admire that. Too much trust can come back to bite us on the ass. There've been times when I got bit but finally I learned my lesson."

Fargo studied the ground without being obvious. He read tracks as easily as some men read books, and these told him a lot.

"Care for a drink? I got some squeezin's I make myself," Rolf offered.

"Why not?" Fargo said.

The mountain man went to the doorway, stooped, and disappeared into the black pitch.

Fargo moved just enough that he wasn't visible from inside.

He heard a clank and rattling and then a thump. "You all right in there?"

Rolf filled the doorway, a jug in his hand. "I ain't the tidiest of gents. My wife likes to say I'm the biggest mess ever born."

"She's here with you?" Fargo said in surprise.

Rolf's features clouded and when he spoke his voice was choked with emotion. "Slip of the tongue. No, she ain't. My Martha went to her reward pretty near five years ago."

"Sorry to hear that."

"Why should you be?" Rolf said. "You didn't know her and you don't know me." Shaking himself, he came out and extended the jug.

"You first."

"Afeared I'll poison you?" Rolf said, and laughed. He leaned the Hawken against the wall, wrestled the stopper out, and crooked his arm. "To trust," he said, and tilted the jug to his mouth. He swallowed a few times and let out a contented sigh. "Your turn."

Fargo wiped it on his left sleeve and took a swig. He figured it would be potent but he didn't count on his mouth and throat filling with liquid fire, or on his eyes watering. "Damn," he said, and coughed. "That stuff would curl a nail."

"I'll take that as a compliment," Rolf said, grinning. He helped himself to the jug.

"You must have an iron gut," Fargo said.

Rolf shrugged between swallows. "I'm used to it. Took to drinkin' a lot after I lost Martha. Too much, I suspect, but I needed to dull the pain."

"How did she die, if you don't mind my asking?"

Rolf seemed to struggle with himself, then said, "I do mind. She's one thing I never talk about. Ever."

"I understand."

"Like hell you do," Rolf said. "But if you'd lost your woman the way I lost mine—" He caught himself. "Listen to me, goin' on and on."

"Getting back to the animals we're hunting," Fargo reminded him. "You say you've only caught a glimpse now and then?"

"You callin' me a liar?"

"I am."

About to take another drink, Rolf lowered the jug. "You better have a damn good reason."

Fargo swept his arm at the dirt under their feet. "I've got dozens of them."

There were tracks everywhere: the old man's tracks, the track of the mules, and the tracks of two animals that weren't wolves and weren't dogs.

Rolf looked down and gave a mild start. "I'll be damned."

"Care to explain?"

"They must have come around when I'm not here."

"That must be it," Fargo said.

"You don't believe me, do you?"

"Not a damn word," Fargo said. "Like you told me, too much trust can bite us on the ass."

"Ain't that the truth." Rolf's hand came from behind his back; he was holding a pocket pistol, and cocked it. "I told you before and I'll tell you again. One twitch and it'll be your last."

35

"Well now," Fargo said.

Rolf raised the pistol and pointed it at Fargo's face. "Let go of the rifle."

Fargo relaxed his fingers and the Henry clattered on the ground.

"Kick it toward me."

Fargo pushed the stock with his toe.

"Two fingers and two fingers only," Rolf said, "take that Colt of yours and let it drop."

Again Fargo complied.

"Move three steps back with your arms out from your sides," Rolf ordered.

Simmering inside, Fargo had no choice but to do as he was told. The muzzle of the pocket pistol never wavered.

Rolf picked up the Henry and the Colt. Backing up, he placed them beside the Hawken. "Now we can talk. Who in blazes are you?"

"I already told you."

"Not your name. What you do. Dressed like that, you sure as hell ain't a cow nurse. And you're not no damned sheepherder. So I ask you again. Who the hell are you, mister? And how are you involved in this?"

Fargo gave him a bare account, ending with, "And here we are."

"A scout and a tracker. That explains it." Rolf let out a loud sigh.

"Suppose you return the favor. What are you up to? And where are they?"

"Have some of it figured out, do you?" Rolf said. "What gave it away?"

"When the sheepherders told me their dogs were killed first."

"You reckoned that someone wanted to keep their dogs from following the scent back?"

"Something like that, yes," Fargo said.

Rolf uttered an odd laugh. "They did the dogs on their own. They hate dogs." He added almost as an afterthought. "They do a lot on their own, damn them. It's the blood. They taste it and go half wild."

"Did you sic them on the little girl?"

Rolf stiffened. "What's that? You say a child was killed?"

"Her name was Angelita. She was ten years old."

"I didn't intend for that."

The mountain man's shock appeared sincere, which added to Fargo's puzzlement. "You let them loose and they do what they want? Is that it?"

"I just told you I can't always control them." Rolf put his other hand to his face. "I didn't mean for it to come to this. It's him I'm after."

"Him who?"

Rolf snapped his arm down. "I've told you too much as it is. He might guess and I don't want him to know until I'm ready to do him in." He wagged the pistol. "Turn around."

Fargo hesitated.

"Mister, I've got no quarrel with you. But I will by God shoot you if you don't do as I tell you."

Fargo believed him. Reluctantly, he slowly turned.

"I planned for too long and have gone to too much trouble to let anyone stop me now. He has this coming, the son of a bitch. Ask him. Ask him about Antelope Springs and see what he says."

The name stirred a vague recollection. Before Fargo could recall why, the back of his head exploded and he was sucked into a black well.

His next sensation was of a hand on his shoulder, shaking him. He struggled up through inner depths and suddenly his eyes were open and his head was throbbing with pain. He squinted in the harsh glare of the sun and looked around in confusion.

Hank was hunkered next to him. Billy-Bob was over by the shack, a hand on his revolver. Their horses and the Ovaro were nearby.

Carlos sat on his animal, smirking.

"That's a nasty bump you got on your noggin," Hank said.

Wincing, Fargo sat up. He touched the back of his head. There was no blood, just the goose egg. His hat had fallen off and he gingerly placed it back on. "How long?"

"Were you out?" Hank said. "It's been over an hour since you came on ahead. We got to worryin' that maybe somethin' had happened. Well, Billy and me. The mutton lover don't give a damn."

"It's good to see you suffering, gringo," Carlos happily declared.

Billy-Bob came over carrying the Henry and the Colt. "These here are yours, ain't they?"

Fargo stood. The pain worsened but he grit his teeth and bore it. He shoved the Colt into his holster and brushed dust from the rifle. "I'm obliged."

"Who was it done this to you?" Hank asked.

"The name Igmar Rolf mean anything to you?"

"Sure don't," Hank said.

"That's a German handle, ain't it?" Billy-Bob asked. "Is he the one who hit you?"

Fargo went to nod but caught himself. Shuffling to the Ovaro, he slid the Henry into the scabbard. "Mount up," he said, and carefully pulled himself onto his saddle. The movement provoked more pain.

"What do you aim to do?" Hank said.

"Find the son of a bitch."

The tracks of the two mules were fresh enough. Rolf had gone south at a gallop.

Fargo used his spurs and endured the torment. For half an hour he pushed and then he slowed to spare their animals. It was obvious catching Rolf would take some doing. Fargo bent to study the mule tracks and gauge how far ahead Rolf was. Abruptly drawing rein, he swore.

"What is it?" Hank asked.

Fargo pointed. "He's not alone."

The cowboys came up.

"I'll be damned," Billy-Bob said.

Imprinted in the dirt were the tracks of the two beasts that had been terrorizing Hermanos Valley.

"Am I readin' this right?" Billy-Bob said. "These things are his pets?"

"Sure looks like it," Hank said.

"What in hell is goin' on, anyhow?" Billy-Bob said.

Fargo wished he knew.

36

They lost the trail on a rocky flat, over a hundred acres of solid rock that barely showed the scratches of shod hooves, and the mules weren't shod. Fargo suspected that Rolf had wrapped pieces of hides over their hooves to make it even harder.

Two hours Fargo spent roving the edge of the flat in the belief that he could find where the tracks took up but he and the others couldn't find a single print.

"It beats all hollow they've licked us," Hank said.

"What do we do now?" Billy-Bob asked.

Carlos answered before Fargo could. "We go back, gringo. We have come all this way and accomplished nothing."

"We know who we're up against now," Hank said. "That's somethin'."

"How about we stake out that shack of his?" Billy-Bob proposed. "He's bound to show up sooner or later."

"You can if you want but I'm going back," Carlos reiterated.

"What put a burr up your ass, sheepman?" Hank said.

"I'm only here because Porfiro made me come," Carlos replied. "As to your question, unlike your friend, I'm not stupid. Do you really think he will return to his hovel now that we know about it? And even if he did, he will have his animals with him. He will wait until night and set them on us in the dark."

"Not if I can help it." Billy-Bob patted his six-shooter. "And who are you callin' stupid, mutton eater?"

Fargo nipped their argument by saying, "We have to go back anyway."

"Why?" Hank asked.

"To warn your boss and the sheepherders. It was one thing when we thought we were up against wild animals. They need to know someone is behind this, and he's out for blood."

No one objected. They had many miles to cover and their horses were tired so they held to a walk most of the way and it was nearly ten that night when they wound down out of the mountains to the valley floor. To the south were the fires of the cowboys, to the north those of the sheepherders.

Fargo and the cowboys stopped but Carlos reined north and broke into a trot.

"We'll go tell Mr. Trask," Hank said. "We'll explain about Shorty, about how he prodded you, but Mr. Trask won't like it none." He touched his hat brim.

Fargo was in no hurry. By the time he reached the wagons, all the men and women were gathered around Porfiro and Carlos, having a heated talk. He went around to the string and tiredly dismounted. As he was untying his bedroll the fragrance of mint wreathed him.

"You're back," Delicia said.

"Miss me?" Fargo joked, and was troubled by her expression.

Delicia kissed him on the cheek and stepped back. "More than you know." She paused. "Do you think you are in the mood tonight?"

"Women," Fargo said.

"What?"

"Nothing." Fargo bent to the cinch.

"Carlos has told us about the . . . what did he call him? Mountain man? Everyone is stunned. Why would he harm us? What have we ever done to him?"

"Ever hear of a place called Antelope Springs?"

"I have not. Why?"

"Ask Porfiro if he has."

"Ask me what, senor?" said their leader, coming over.

Fargo put the same question to him.

"No, senor, I have not," Porfiro said. "Of what importance is it?"

"I don't know yet," Fargo admitted.

Porfiro cleared his throat. "I have a question of my own. Carlos says the cowboys tried to kill him and you stopped them. Is that true?"

"They hung him from a tree. I don't think they aimed to do him in."

"But *you* killed one of *them*?"

"Don't remind me." Fargo slid the saddle off and held it over his shoulder.

"This is bad," Porfiro said. "You are our friend so they might blame us in some way. I would avoid trouble if I can. Perhaps I should go talk to this Trask."

"It's best you leave it be," Fargo advised.

"I don't know," Porfiro said uncertainly.

"Us gringos have a saying," Fargo said. "Cross that bridge when you come to it." He walked past and went to the wagon and swung his saddle under. They followed him.

"Everything has become so complicated," Porfiro lamented. "All we ever wanted was to be left alone."

"Life does that," Fargo said.

"Does what, senor?"

"Kicks us in the teeth when we least expect."

"Perhaps you can—" Porfiro began, and stopped, his mouth half open.

From off the high slopes to the east came the familiar ululating cry. Pregnant with savage menace, it seemed to hang on the very air.

"*Madre de Dios,*" Porfiro exclaimed. "It is back."

"*They* are back," Fargo corrected him.

"That's right. Carlos told us there are two Hounds. As if one wasn't calamity enough."

Delicia broke her silence with, "Now that we know about *el hombre de Montana*, you would think he would go away."

"Not him," Fargo said. "He's out for blood. I doubt he'll stop this side of the grave."

"Are you saying the only way to stop him is to kill him, senor?"

"As dead as dead can be."

37

The sheepherders reminded Fargo of folks at a funeral waiting for the casket to be lowered into the ground. They sat around in a glum mood, talking in low tones and casting anxious glances into the dark whenever a bray wafted up the valley.

"The beasts are at the south end tonight," Delicia said. "Let's hope they stay there."

Fargo would like a shot at the brutes but not at the expense of more lives. "I'm tempted to go after them."

"Whatever for? The cowboys don't trust you. Give them an excuse, any excuse, and they'll turn on you."

"Please, senor," Porfiro said. "I beg you to stay with us. We have little experience with matters like this."

"And you think I do?"

A wagon door slammed and out lurched Carlos with a bottle of wine. He tilted it to his lips and gulped, spilling some down his chin. Wearing a vicious grin, he swaggered among his people, heedless of the looks of disapproval.

The wagon door opened again and Constanza hastened after him. She put a hand on his arm and tried to stop him but he smacked her arm away.

"Look at how he acts," Porfiro said. "The blood of my blood."

"Brother, please," Delicia said as Carlos came to their fire.

"Shut up," Carlos snapped. Glaring at Fargo, he swallowed more wine. "Don't think I've forgotten about you, gringo."

"Carlos, stop," Porfiro said.

"You can shut up too, old man," Carlos said. "This is between the gringo and me."

"You embarrass all of us," Porfiro said.

"No more than you embarrass me, Grandfather," Carlos

retorted. "Bending over backwards to those miserable cowboys. You sicken me."

Constanza touched his elbow. "Enough of this, grandson. For once my husband is right. Behave yourself."

"I'll behave, all right," Carlos said, and swept his serape aside. A revolver was in his waistband.

"Carlos, no!" Delicia said. She stood and sought to snatch the six-shooter but he pushed her away.

"What do you think you are up to?" Porfiro demanded.

"Look at my face." Carlos fumed. "This gringo pig has beat on me, twice. I look in the mirror and I am reminded of it. But no more."

Porfiro rose and moved between Fargo and his grandson. "You've had too much to drink. Go back into the wagon and sleep it off."

"Move, old man," Carlo said.

"Don't use that tone with me."

A man at another fire hollered, "Do as your grandfather tells you, boy."

"Stay out of this!" Carlos raged. "All of you." He glued his mouth to the bottle but it was empty and after shaking it, he threw it down and swore.

"Carlos, please," Delicia pleaded.

"I do not forget an insult." Carlos splayed his fingers over the revolver. "On your feet, gringo. Or I will kill you where you sit."

"Enough," Porfiro said. He placed his hands on Carlos' arms and tried to push him toward the wagon.

"Yes, enough," Carlos said, and suddenly backhanding his grandfather across the face, he took a step back, drew the revolver, and shot Porfiro in the chest.

Delicia screamed.

Constanza clutched at her throat.

Everyone else, from oldest to youngest, was rooted in shock and disbelief.

Not Fargo. He drew and threw himself to the right just as Carlos pointed the pistol at him and fired. The slug dug a furrow in the spot where Fargo had been sitting. Prone on his side, Fargo shot Carlos in the forehead. The rear of Carlos' cranium exploded and the lifeless body, animated by a brief last spark, tottered a couple of steps and buckled, oozing into a pile of disjointed limbs.

Fargo slowly got to his feet. Gun smoke rose from the muzzle of the Colt as he replaced the spent cartridge.

No one else moved. No one else spoke.

Delicia broke the spell. She let out a wail and threw herself on her brother and sobbed.

Constanza stumbled to Porfiro and sank silently beside him, tears pouring.

And now others were up and coming to comfort them. The few glances thrown at Fargo were cold and resentful. He went around the fire and over to Porfiro's wagon. He still had half a mind to mount up and go but he couldn't accomplish much in the dark so he slipped underneath and spread out his bedroll.

The whole camp was in anguish over their loss. Half a dozen women were weeping and more than a few children. An old man kept yelling to the stars, "Why, Lord? Why?"

Fargo rolled onto his side. He thought maybe he wouldn't be able to drift off but in no time he was under and slept as deeply as a baby. His last thought before sleep claimed him was about Carlos; he should have shot the son of a bitch days ago.

38

The first thing Fargo noticed when he opened his eyes at the crack of dawn was the silence. Usually a few of the sheepherders were already up and there would be the clink of breakfast dishes or the ding of a spoon against a pot and the crackle of a fire or two. But this morning there was the absolute quiet of a cemetery.

Puzzled, Fargo rolled onto his back. He was about to put his hat on when he noticed the second thing that was strange. The wagon was completely surrounded by legs and feet. The legs of men, the legs of women, even the legs of children. Jamming his hat on, he poked his head out from under.

"We have been waiting for you to wake up," Constanza said.

Fargo gripped the edge of the wagon and levered out from underneath. Only one face was the least bit friendly—Delicia's, and she was standing well back. Apparently she had been told to.

"What's this?" Fargo asked.

"As if you can't guess," Constanza returned. "We've been up all night. We buried our dead, and then we held a council. It was about you."

"Bet it was your idea," Fargo said.

She smiled. "Can you guess the decision we came to?"

"Too much guessing this early in the day," Fargo said. "Why don't you come out with it? I can tell you can hardly hold it in."

"You are the most despicable man I have ever met."

"And you're the biggest bitch. So we're even."

Muttering broke out. Expressions became darker and a few of the men balled their fists.

"I have not liked you from the beginning," Constanza said. "I begged Porfiro to make you leave but he felt you could help us. And look at where it got him."

"You can't blame me for that," Fargo said.

"But I can. If you had left, none of this would have happened. My grandson would not have been humiliated, and would not have gotten drunk and sought revenge."

"It's my fault he was a jackass?"

"Don't speak ill of the dead," Constanza said harshly. "Have you no decency?"

"More than you ever will."

"How dare you?" Constanza said.

For a few moments Fargo thought she was going to strike him but she controlled herself and folded her arms across her scrawny bosom.

"No. I will not stoop to your level. But I have a few things to say." Constanza's mouth compressed into a slit. "You have cost me my husband, the man I spent more than fifty years of my life with. You have cost me my grandson, whom I adored. In my heart I grieve, in my soul I am stricken."

Fargo didn't say anything.

"We have talked it over, all the elders, and we have decided that you have brought nothing but pain and sorrow to our people. We do not want you here. We want to you pack your things and saddle your animal and leave." Constanza paused. "And we want you to do it right this instant."

"I don't get a cup of coffee first?"

"Be thankful you leave with your life," Constanza said. "Were it entirely up to me, you wouldn't."

"I gave your husband my word I'd track down the things that have killed your people and your sheep."

"He is dead. And your word means nothing to the rest of us. I say again, go."

"What about the cowboys?"

"What about them?" Constanza countered. "We do not need your help with them, either."

"They'll drive you out of this valley."

"They only think they will," Constanza said. "We have made plans to deal with them." She gazed at the rising sun. "We will give you ten minutes. If you are not gone by then, we will assist you, and we won't be gentle about it."

"You're enjoying this," Fargo said.

"Yes, I am," Constanza admitted. "Not as much as I would

enjoy having your throat slit, or having you shot. I would have had you cast out well before this if not for Porfiro."

"He was a good man."

"Yes, he was."

"What he saw in you I'll never savvy."

"You go too far," Constanza said. "And you squander your ten minutes." She gestured, and a path was opened from the wagon to the string.

To argue any further was pointless. Fargo carried his saddle blanket and saddle to the Ovaro. He rolled up his blankets and tied them on his bedroll. He shoved the Henry into the scabbard, and was ready. Stepping into the stirrups, he looked down on them, lingering his gaze on Delicia and Yoana. "You're on your own from here on out."

"As we wish to be," Constanza said, and motioned. "Your ten minutes are about up."

"Hell of a start to a day," Fargo said, and headed south.

He hadn't gone twenty yards when he passed the fresh graves.

39

Fargo missed not having coffee. He could go without food but he liked to start his mornings with three or four piping hot cups.

He had ridden about a mile when his craving got the better of him. Reining into the timber, he climbed to a flat spot and dismounted. He gathered downed limbs and broke them and used his fire steel and flint to kindle a fire. Once the flames were high enough, he emptied half his canteen into his coffeepot and unwrapped his coffee grounds.

Soon a familiar pleasant aroma heightened his craving.

There was an old saying to the effect that a watched pot never boiled but he was watching his and he was pleased when he finally held his battered tin cup in both hands and sipped. He didn't need sugar or milk. The coffee alone sufficed.

Rosy sunlight had spread over Hermanos Valley. It belied the dark underbelly.

Fargo was on his second cup when he sensed someone or something was behind him. He started to draw and turn but a muzzle was thrust practically in his face. Staring into the Hawken, he smiled and said, "Morning."

"Your smoke gave you away," Igmar Rolf said.

Fargo scanned the vegetation. "Where are your pets? I didn't think you went anywhere without them."

"I don't," Rolf said.

"I'd like to see them," Fargo said as casually as if he were making small talk with a friend. "And find out why you hate the Bar T so much."

Rolf came around and hunkered, careful to stay out of reach. "How did you know?"

"You and your pets showed up about the same time they did. Either you were working with them or you were after them."

"I'm out to ruin Ben Trask. I wanted my pets to only kill his cows but they'd rather kill sheep."

"And ten-year-old girls," Fargo said.

"That was an accident."

"They're your animals. It's on your shoulders."

"You might be surprised to hear I accept the blame."

"Damned decent of you."

"Spare me your spite," Rolf said. "If you knew my story, you'd be on my side."

"Tell me about Antelope Springs," Fargo prompted, and drank more coffee to give the impression he was content to talk and nothing else.

"Why should I?"

"I'm curious what Trask did," Fargo said. "What could drive a man to do what you're doing?"

Rolf was quiet awhile. Finally he said, "A hundred miles or so southeast of here is a small valley. A lot like this one. There's plenty of grass and a lot of woodland and a couple of springs. Hence, Antelope Springs." His face clouded with emotion. "It was my valley, Fargo. I was there long before other whites, and I'd lived there for nigh on thirty years. Then one day Mr. Benjamin Trask showed up. He was always on the lookout for new graze, he said, and he intended to make Antelope Springs his."

"The same as here. What did you say?"

"I told him to go to hell and take his cows with him."

"He's not the tail-tucking kind," Fargo said.

"I found that out a month later. Him and his hands struck in the middle of the night. They threw torches on our cabin. I shot a few and then a beam fell on my Martha."

"That's how you lost your wife?"

Rolf didn't seem to hear him. "It made me half crazy and I ran outside and they shot me."

"You're lucky to be breathing."

"Luck, hell," Rolf spat. "Six or seven of 'em put lead into me. They thought I was dead. They burned my cabin and shot my mule and tore down my corral and left me lyin' there in a pool of blood."

"Damn," Fargo said.

"So now you know."

"Not all of it. It's taken you awhile to come after them."

"I crawled off into the hills and laid low. Took me more than a year to heal to where I could walk without a crutch. I wasn't thinkin' about revenge then. I wasn't thinkin' about anythin' except how much I missed Martha. I took to drinkin' and not carin'."

"What brought you out of it?"

Rolf's lips quirked in a strange smile. "A wolf."

"The tracks I've seen, the animal I saw, isn't a wolf," Fargo said.

Rolf idly tugged at his beard. "I reckon I might as well tell you the rest. It was a wolf pup. The ma got shot. Not by me. Probably a hunter. When I found them, the pup was lyin' next to the body, whimperin'. I took it in and cared for it. It was a female and I named her Martha after my wife."

Fargo rested his elbows on his knees. He was all interest.

"Not long after, I went to a settlement for supplies. A man had a litter of pups he was givin' away. I don't know what made me do it but I took one, a male. Called him Caleb. He and Martha ran together, played together, ate together. She was about two years old when it happened."

"She had pups of her own and Caleb was the father," Fargo said.

Igmar Rolf nodded. "I didn't know wolves and dogs could breed together. Guess you'd call the mix a mongrel but they were nothin' like their ma or their pa. They were god-awful big, and god-awful mean."

"How many in the litter?"

"Five."

"You've got two with you," Fargo noted. "What happened to the rest?"

"One was bit by a rattler and died when it wasn't but six months old. Another got kicked by one of my mules when it nipped at her legs and had its head stove in. The third went off one day and never came back. That left Goliath and Esther." Rolf gazed past him. "Their names are from the Bible. I can't read a lick but Martha could. She'd read from it every evenin'."

"I sure would like to see them," Fargo said.

Rolf grinned. "Then turn around."

Fargo started to—and from behind him came a menacing growl.

40

"Do it slow," Igmar Rolf said, "or you might get your head bit off."

The thing was huge. A mix of wolf and dog traits but twice the size of any wolf or dog that ever lived, its eyes blazed with feral intelligence and its lips were drawn back to bare slavering fangs. Its thick legs, its protuberant muscles, added to its bulk and the impression of raw ferocity.

Behind it and to one side was a slightly smaller version, not as bulky, and shaggier.

"Meet Goliath and Esther," Rolf introduced them.

Fargo smiled at the big one and it growled. "Not all that friendly, are they?"

"The only human they'll come anywhere near is me."

Fargo stared into Goliath's piercing eyes and imagined those fangs ripping the throat out of ten-year-old Angelita.

"And you can't control them all that well."

"No," Rolf admitted. "It's as I told you. I wanted them to only kill the cowboys and Trask's cows but they do as they please. And it seems like they enjoy killin' sheep more."

"Do you have any idea what you've done?"

"I'm out to get the son of a bitch who killed my wife. Nothin' else matters."

Goliath suddenly took a step closer, his hackles rising.

Fargo's right hand was inches from his Colt. He might be able to get off a shot; he might not.

"Down, boy," Rolf said. "Leave him be."

Goliath crouched as if to spring.

"See what I mean?" Rolf said. Rising, he stepped around Fargo and placed his hand on the wolf dog's neck. "I won't let him hurt you provided you give me your word."

"About what?"

"I have nothin' against you, mister," Rolf said. "It's Trask

I'm after. So if you give me your word that you'll light a shuck and never come back, you're free to go."

Fargo thought of Delicia and Yoana. "What about the sheepherders?"

"What are they to you?"

"How many of them will your pets kill before this is over?"

"How can I predict?" Rolf shrugged. "They are half wild, after all."

"Then I'm not going anywhere," Fargo said.

Rolf sighed. "I gave you credit for more sense."

Fargo had made up his mind. He didn't give a damn about Trask and hardly gave a damn about any of the sheepherders except for Delicia but he couldn't let any more little girls be killed. He was confident he could draw and put a slug into the old mountain man before Rolf could fire but shooting him wouldn't solve the worse problem of the wolf dogs. Without their master, they'd likely wander all over, killing as they went. There was no telling how many folks they'd rip apart. So the way he saw it, he had to put an end to them—right here and now.

Accordingly, Fargo set down his tin cup and made as if to reach for the coffeepot to refill it but as his hand rose he filled it with the Colt and pivoted on his boot heels toward Goliath and Esther.

Rolf was more alert than he counted on, and saw him draw. "At him!" he bawled, pointing.

It was the command to attack.

Fargo didn't quite have the Colt level when Goliath sprang.

Those slavering jaws snapped at his face even as the brute's heavy body slammed into his chest. Fargo was knocked onto his back with the giant wolf dog on top of him. He rammed his left forearm against the animal's throat but it had no effect.

Again Goliath snapped at him, and he shot it.

Goliath howled and bounded back.

Esther crouched to leap at him.

Scrambling to his knees, Fargo took aim to be sure and paid for the moment's delay with an explosion of pain in the side of his head. The world spun and he pitched forward. He experienced a fleeting instant of dread in which he imagined the wolf dogs tearing into him while he was helpless, and then the bright sunlight blinked to black. He wasn't out long, though. He opened his eyes and heard crashing in the undergrowth and Rolf bellowing at the top of his lungs.

"Goliath! Come back! Heel, boy! Come to me!"

Fargo lurched to his feet, stumbled to the Ovaro, and yanked the Henry from the scabbard. He needed to go after them but his legs wouldn't work. He managed a few halting steps and stopped to let his head clear.

He was lucky Rolf hadn't finished him off. The mountain man had gone off after his pet and the other one had gone with him.

Scarlet drops led into the trees, so he knew he'd hit Goliath. The question was, would it kill him?

Fargo tested his legs, raising and lowering first one and then the other. He was about to plunge into the woods when he stopped short and blurted, "What the hell am I doing?" Quickly, he climbed on the Ovaro and went in pursuit. The crashing had faded and Rolf had stopped shouting. He rode in the direction he thought they had gone but after fifty yards, he stopped. He hadn't come across a single track. Reining to the north, he commenced a search. Every minute of delay increased their chances of getting away, and after fifteen minutes he was forced to admit they had.

Fargo returned to the fire. He hated to let good coffee go to waste but he upended the pot and doused the flames. Winding down to the valley floor, he wheeled the stallion to the south.

It was a long ride to the far end of the valley but he was spared from having to go that far. He was about halfway there when he galloped around a bend and nearly rode into hundreds of grazing cows.

Fargo drew rein. The cows were being pushed north by Bar T hands. The point riders and two of the swing riders spotted him and converged.

Griff Wexler was one of the point riders. The swing riders were Billy-Bob and Hank.

Griff drew rein and demanded, "What the hell are you doin' here?"

"I need to talk to your boss."

"You've got your nerve after what you did to Shorty."

"He was on the prod," Fargo said, and looked at Billy-Bob and Hank, surprised they hadn't explained the shooting to Trask and the rest of the hands.

"I wish you hadn't of come," Billy-Bob said.

"Mr. Trask is powerful mad at you," Hank remarked.

"I have to see him," Fargo said. "It's important."

"Oh, we'll take you to him, all right," Griff Wexler said. "But you're goin' to wish we hadn't."

41

Ben Trask wasn't one of those ranchers who let their hands do all the work. He was riding flank.

As Fargo was escorted around the herd, other cowboys joined them, so that by the time they reached Trask, he was surrounded by eleven punchers.

Trask leaned on his saddle horn and waited. His expression didn't give anything away. But the first words out of his mouth did. "I should thank you, scout. You've spared me the trouble of huntin' you down."

"If it's about Shorty—" Fargo started to say.

"I warned you," Trask said. "No one hurts my men except they answer to me. Hurt one, and you get hurt. Kill one, and you're as good as dead."

"Damn it, Trask. Listen."

"I'm through listenin' to you, mister. You and your talk about bein' reasonable, about lettin' those mutton lovers share the valley with us. And then you go and shoot one of my hands."

"He was trying to shoot me."

"So Billy-Bob and Hank told me. But Shorty was under orders not to cause trouble and that boy always did exactly what I told him. No, you shot him to protect the worst of the sheepmen, that Carlos."

Fargo was losing his patience and his temper. "I shot Carlos, too."

"What?"

"He killed Porfiro and I killed him and now the sheepherders don't want anything to do with me."

"Carlos is dead?" Billy-Bob said, and laughed. "I reckon it couldn't happen to a nicer feller."

"Amen to that," Hank said. "If I wasn't so peaceable by nature, I'd have shot him my own self."

Trask hadn't taken his eyes off Fargo. "It doesn't change anythin'. You still have to answer for Shorty."

"And you have to answer for Antelope Springs."

Ben Trask stiffened. So did Griff Wexler and several of his punchers. They all looked at one another.

"What's Antelope Springs, boss?" Billy-Bob asked.

"It was before you hired on," Trask said gruffly. Abruptly reining away, he snapped over his shoulder, "Fargo, you come with me. We need to talk."

"I should go too," Griff said.

"No. Keep drivin' the herd. We're not stoppin' until this whole valley is our graze."

Fargo followed, his hand on his Colt. If the rancher went for his revolver, there'd be another body to bury.

Trask rode to the tree line, swung around so his back was to the forest, and drew rein. Taking a crumpled bandanna from a pocket, he moped at the sweat on his face and said thickly, "All right. How in hell do you know about Antelope Springs? More to the point, *what* do you know?"

"I know you didn't learn your lesson," Fargo said. "You're doing the same thing here you did there."

"So? Antelope Valley has been part of the Bar T for years now."

"And has come back to bite you on the ass," Fargo said. "Igmar Rolf is still alive."

The rancher's amazement was almost comical. "That's impossible. We shot him to pieces."

"Then you admit it? You killed his wife and then you gunned the old man down."

"Old man, hell!" Trask practically roared. "He might look old but he's as spry as you or me. And the most stubborn coot who ever drew breath." Trask swore luridly. "Is that what he told you? That I was to blame?"

"You had your men throw torches on their cabin."

"To drive him and his wife out. But the son of a bitch wouldn't come. I could hear his wife yellin' at him to throw down his rifle and step out with his hands in the air, like I told him to do, but he refused. He waited until the cabin was fallin' in on itself, and then he came out with his rifle blazin'. We had to shoot to defend ourselves."

"The same with me and Shorty."

If Trask heard him, he didn't give any sign. He had gone on. "I'll bet that bastard didn't tell you all of it. How I offered him twice what his homestead was worth but he wouldn't take it."

"A man has a right to live where he wants."

"Not when he's killin' and eatin' my beeves, he doesn't. He was too lazy to go off into the mountains after game and took to eatin' my cows. Back then my range was near the valley he lived in but I didn't need it and left him be. Did he tell you that? Did he tell you how my punchers kept findin' slaughtered cows? I had a suspicion it was him so to stop the killin' I offered to buy him out and he told me to go to hell."

"So you decided to drive him out and his wife died."

"As God is my witness," Trask said solemnly, "I never meant for her to come to harm."

Fargo believed him.

"Now you say he's back?"

"And he has two pets," Fargo revealed. "Part wolf, part dog, and all mean. It's them we've been hearing at night."

"Hold on, now," Trask said. "If Rolf is after me, why have his pets been killin' the sheepherders and their sheep?"

"He can't control them as much as he'd like to."

"Oh hell. That sounds like somethin' that addlepated old bastard would do."

"It's what I came to tell you," Fargo said, "and to ask you one last time to let the sheepherders alone."

"I can't. The Bar T has grown so much, I need this graze. I'm sorry, but there's nothin' you can do."

"Yes," Fargo said, and loosened the Colt in its holster, "there is."

Trask's eyes became twin points of flint. "Are you threatenin' me? Because if you are, you'll find that I don't kowtow to anyone. I'm not scared of you and I'm not scared of that old buzzard, either."

Fargo glimpsed movement in the woods over Trask's shoulder.

A buckskin-clad figure materialized with the Hawken to his shoulder. Before he could shout a warning, the Hawken belched lead and smoke.

Ben Trask's face burst in a gout of flesh, bone and blood.

42

Fargo started to draw but as he was clearing leather a piece of flesh struck him on the right cheek near his eye. In reflex he recoiled and grabbed at it, and Igmar Rolf melted into the vegetation.

Trask's heavy body keeled from the saddle and hit the ground with a thud.

Fargo went to rein around Trask's horse and go after the mountain man. He heard shouts from the cowboys and then he was in the forest. To the north came the crash of brush to the passage of a large animal. He caught sight of Rolf on a mule, flying at a gallop, and gave chase.

With all the trees and thickets and boulders, Fargo couldn't gain. He became aware of streaks of gray-brown on either side of the mule: Goliath and Esther, the wolf dogs.

He wondered why Rolf was fleeing north instead of east. For half a mile the mule proved remarkably fleet. Unexpectedly, Rolf reined to the west, toward the valley floor—and the herd.

Fargo angled to cut the mountain man off but he was too far behind. By the time the Ovaro pounded into the open, Rolf and the wolf dogs had reached the cattle.

Punchers were farther back and up ahead but none were close enough to stop him.

Fearsome brays pierced the air. Goliath and Esther sprang in among the cows, biting and clawing and wreaking havoc.

Igmar Rolf whooped and waved his Hawken.

Fargo raised his Colt to shoot. The mountain man's intent was obvious, and he had to stop him. But the harm had been done. The savage howls of the wolf dogs, the mooing and bleats of stricken cows, the whooping and the hollering and the commotion, sent a wave of fear through the herd. As if possessed of one mind, they broke into motion.

"Stampede!" a cowboy hollered. "My God, the critters are stampedin'!"

Fargo had witnessed stampedes before. Docile herds were turned into raging rivers of destruction, their hammering hooves leveling everything in their path.

"Stop them!" a puncher screamed.

"Turn the leaders!" another cried.

It was too late for that. The thousands of head were fleeing pell-mell up the valley.

Fargo was fortunate that he was twenty yards from them when they broke. Or so he thought until he glanced to the south and discovered that the tail of the herd was stampeding, too, and sweeping wide as they came. A spreading line of heads and horns was coming straight at him.

Hauling on the reins, Fargo made for the timber. A cowboy south of him was trying to do the same but the leading wave of beeves slammed into him and his horse like a storm-tossed breaker on the Pacific shore. Fargo would never forget the squeal of the puncher's horse and the man's death wail.

The din assaulted Fargo's ears. He rode for his life, the ground under the stallion quaking. He still had the Colt in his hand; he could shoot one or two but what good would that do? He jabbed his spurs and prayed.

Dust filled his nose and he tasted it on his tongue. Somewhere a man shrieked. He hoped it was Igmar Rolf, that the mountain man had been killed by his own hate.

The living wall of death was almost on him. Another jab of his spurs, and the stallion plowed into the forest heedless of the limbs that scratched and tore.

Behind Fargo a raging phalanx of cows thundered past. He stopped and turned in the saddle and watched the brutes streaming up the valley. They would run for miles, maybe clear to the north end.

The thought jarred him.

"God, no."

Fargo reined north and came to a gallop. He stayed in the trees. He had no choice. The valley floor was covered with cows. There was no way he could get ahead of the herd and try to turn them.

His horsemanship was put to the test. Constantly reining right and left to avoid oaks and pines and boulders, he paralleled the herd. They passed the midway point and thundered around a bend. Terror-struck sheep fled.

The sheepherders would hear the stampede, Fargo told himself, and head for the high timber. If not—he refused to think about that.

From the front of the herd came shots, a cowboy making a desperate bid to stop the dreadnought of hooves and horns, Fargo reckoned. He wasn't surprised that it didn't work. Nothing would stop these cows short of exhaustion.

Since he couldn't stop them it made no sense to ride the Ovaro into the ground. And he had to see for himself if his worst fear came true.

Fargo angled up the mountain. He had to climb a quarter of a mile before he could see the wagons in the far distance. He drew rein, and swore.

The campfires still burned, and figures were moving about.

Half a mile or more separated the onrushing herd from the camp. There was plenty of time yet for the sheepherders to flee. He could just make out the horse string and saw two or three people running to mount. The rest formed at the south end of the camp and stood there.

"What the hell are you doing?" Fargo said out loud. The glint of sunlight on metal gave him the answer.

Men with guns were going to try to turn the cows. They moved in front of the rest and formed a skirmish line.

"Damn it to hell, you fools," Fargo railed at the wind. There weren't enough of them. But they didn't know that. They were used to dealing with sheep and a sheep stampede was nothing like a cow stampede. It was akin to comparing a flowing stream after a gentle summer rain and the same stream in raging flood. "Get out of there."

The herd had reduced the gap by a quarter mile when several of the wagons lurched into motion, heading for the woodland that rose to the north. But they moved so slowly, they were turtles on wheels.

Fargo imagined Delicia on one of the wagons. He clenched his fists so hard, his nails dug into his palms.

The cattle were running flat-out. Nothing could stop them; nothing could stem the inevitable.

A lot of people were about to die.

43

The line of men with rifles and revolvers moved farther from the wagon, no doubt thinking that they should turn the herd a safe distance from their loved ones.

The flowing legion of hooves and horns was almost on them when the sheepherders fired a volley. From Fargo's vantage, it appeared that they shot in the air. It had no effect. The cattle swept down on them and Fargo heard the crack of several more shots. He heard faint screams, too, as the men went down under the crushing weight and failing hooves.

Until the last instant Fargo hoped against hope that the cows would go around the wagons. They didn't. They engulfed them. Wagons buckled or were smashed onto their sides.

Stick figures tried to run but they were much too slow. In a twinkling the bovine tide washed over them. Screams rose.

Thick smoke coiled from the trampled fires.

Fargo could only imagine the bedlam, and the blood. He saw one of the fleeing wagons veer sharply toward the woods in a bid to escape destruction only to be overtaken. The lead cows parted to go around on either side but the press of numbers forced those behind them to crash into the wagon. A wheel came off and the wagon canted. Faint above the rumble rose a shriek of terror. With a tremendous splintering of wood, the wagon broke apart.

The cattle reached the forest at the valley's end and in a massive sweep of motion, they flowed to the west along the forest's edge and on toward the south again. They only went a short way when they started to slow, their fear and panic subsiding at long last.

Fargo had seen enough. Descending to the valley floor, he used his spurs. He hadn't gone more than a few hundred yards when he came on a puncher who had been caught in the stampede—or what was left of him. The puncher's clothes were ripped and shredded; the man in the clothes was a scarlet sack of bones and ruptured skin.

Fargo came on another and then a third. He passed more dead sheep than he cared to count, and more than a few dead cows.

Several buzzards were circling over the north end of the valley when he got there. Somehow the carrion eaters always knew when a feast was on the table.

The sheepherders in the skirmish line had died horrible deaths. Their mangled remains was enough to churn anyone's stomach.

The camp was worse.

Bodies, or what was left of them, were everywhere—men, women, children.

Dismounting, Fargo roved among the slaughtered. Few were recognizable; faces had been stove in, heads had been split apart. Here and there lay body parts; a finger, a bloody tooth, part of a nose.

A pair of female legs jutted from under a wagon on its side. The wagon had split apart, revealing the head and shoulders of the woman the wagon fell on. It was Constanza, her mouth agape, the whites of her eyes turned red from burst blood vessels.

"Bitch," Fargo said. He took a few more steps, and stopped.

Off in the trees someone was quietly sobbing and sniffling.

"Who's in there?" Fargo called out.

Sheepherders appeared, seven, eight, nine, some stumbling in shock, others weeping. Lorenzo was among them, comforting a woman.

"Is that all of you?" Fargo asked as they straggled into the sunlight.

"There are a few more, I think, senor," Lorenzo said numbly, and motioned with his thumb behind him.

A man limped around a spruce. His clothes were a mess and his cheek was swollen, and he was using a tree limb as an improvised crutch.

An older woman trailed after him, hugging herself and weeping.

Then it was a young woman, a child in her arms, the girl's

face buried in her shoulder. Tears moistened the woman's cheeks. She came to him and said in relief, "I thought perhaps you were dead."

"Thought the same about you, Delicia," Fargo said, annoyed at how his throat constricted.

The little girl stirred and straightened and looked at him with eyes sad beyond her tender years.

"Yoana," Fargo said.

"It was terrible," Yoana said, and sniffled. "My mother and my father—" She couldn't go on, and her face sank to Delicia's shoulder again.

Delicia put her forehead to Fargo's chest and closed her eyes. "We barely made it."

Fargo enfolded them in his arms. "The one who did this will pay," he vowed.

Delicia drew back and stared at the carnage in bleak sorrow. "Small consolation. I wish that—" She stopped and gazed past him. "Oh no. Not them. Not now."

Griff Wexler and fifteen or sixteen cowboys were coming up the valley.

"What can they want?"

"I'll find out," Fargo said. "Get everyone back into the trees."

It didn't take much urging. One look at the cowboys and the sheepherders were quick to seek cover.

Fargo moved out to where the skirmish line had been and waited with his thumbs hooked in his gun belt. If the punchers aimed to do the survivors harm, they'd have to answer to him—in blood.

44

Caked with dust, their clothes damp with sweat, their faces grim, the Bar T hands slowed and spread out. Griff Wexler was out in front, Billy-Bob on his right, Hank on his left.

Fargo let them get within a dozen yards when he announced, "That's close enough."

Griff drew rein and the others followed suit. "Wondered what happened to you."

"I'm wondering what you're doing here," Fargo said.

"We came to see how they made out," Griff said with a nod at the devastated encampment.

"Is that all?" Fargo asked suspiciously.

"And to help if we can."

"You hate sheepherders."

"I hate sheep," Griff said, "and I admit I'm not fond of those who raise them. But there were women and kids here, and I'm not heartless."

"Me either," Billy-Bob said.

Hank nodded in agreement.

The cowboys were worn and tired from their efforts to stem the stampede. One puncher had taken a horn in the leg and his crude bandage was bright crimson. Another had his arm in a sling.

"How many did you lose?"

"We're still lookin' for bodies but eight so far," Griff said somberly. "Five more are back at our camp, so busted up they can't ride."

"It caught us off guard, those cows spookin' like they done," Billy-Bob said.

"What happened, exactly?" Griff Wexler asked. "Hank, here, says he saw Mr. Trask get shot but it wasn't you who shot him. And the next we knew, there was all that damn howlin'."

Fargo imparted all of it: Antelope Valley, Igmar Rolf and his wife, Trask burning the cabin down, and the wolf dogs.

"I remember that old bastard," Griff said when he was done. "Here all these years we figured he was dead."

"He killed our boss and started the stampede deliberate?" Billy-Bob said, and patted his six-gun. "Then I reckon we know what we have to do, don't we?"

The rest of the hands nodded or voiced their assent.

"What I think is—" Griff began, and glanced sharply at the woods.

The sheepherders were coming out of hiding. Slowly, cautiously, they converged on Fargo and stood behind him as if for protection.

"Have they come to finish us off?" Delicia asked.

Griff Wexler flinched. "We're right sorry, ma'am. We'd of driven you out, sure, but not like this."

Billy-Bob doffed his hat and showed most of his teeth. "How do you do, miss. Anythin' we can do for you, all you have to do is ask."

"We could use a fire and food for the children," Delicia said.

Fargo stood back as the cowboys scrambled to help. In short order two fires were crackling and a pot of coffee was perking and Griff Wexler had passed out jerky from his saddlebags.

"We have flour and such in our cook wagon," the foreman informed them. "You're welcome to come for supper if you'd like. All of you, that is."

"I'll round up horses for them to ride," Hank volunteered.

Fargo was glad the two sides were finally getting along. It freed him to do something else. "I'll leave you to it," he said. "I'm going after Igmar Rolf."

"Not alone you're not," Billy-Bob said.

"It was our boss he bucked out in gore," Griff said. "Our cows he stampeded."

"It could take days." Fargo would rather go alone but he supposed they had a right to be in it.

"Mister," Griff said, "we'll hunt that son of a bitch to the ends of the earth, if need be." He turned to Delicia and said, "I beg your pardon, ma'am, for my language."

"That is quite all right, Senor Wexler," Delicia said. "By all means, hunt the son of a bitch down."

The foreman laughed. "It's settled then."

"Not quite," Fargo said. "I'll take three of you along, no more."

"Why not most of us?"

"We'd raise so much dust he'd spot us from miles off," Fargo said, shaking his head. "Three and only three and that's final." He added, "Besides, don't you have a lot of cows to round up?"

"God, do we," Billy-Bob said.

"All right." Griff gave in. "It'll be me and two I pick. How soon do you want to head out?"

"Five minutes ago."

"So soon?" Delicia said.

"Rolf's got more than an hour's head start on us as it is." Fargo turned and walked to the Ovaro and she came with him.

Yoana had fallen asleep, her cheek on Delicia's shoulder. "It will be very dangerous, will it not?"

"It'll be him or us," Fargo said.

"That doesn't answer my question."

"It sure as hell does." Fargo disliked her making a fuss.

"You do this for us after how we treated you?" Delicia said.

"I do it for me," Fargo said. "He tried to kill me and damn near split my head open."

"So you think only of yourself? Is that what you would have me believe?"

"Believe what you want." Fargo took the Ovaro's reins in hand.

Delicia touched his chest and softly asked, "Why are you being so gruff with me?"

"I don't need this. *You* don't need this."

"We share a bond, you and I."

"Hell," Fargo said.

"You will come back, *si*? After you have dealt with this

Rolf?" Delicia kissed him on the cheek. "I would like it very much."

"There are days," Fargo said, and sighed.

"Senor?"

Fargo smiled and touched her on the chin. "I aim to please, ma'am."

"I'm happy to hear it," Delicia said.

45

Fargo had no trouble finding the area where Igmar Rolf and the wolf dogs had attacked the herd, but finding where Rolf went from there proved frustrating. The stampede had obliterated the mule's tracks. He spent the rest of the day going along the edge of the forest to the east.

"Nothin'?" Billy-Bob said when Fargo drew rein and swore.

Griff Wexler and a puncher by the name of Jeffers were behind them.

"Sun's almost down," Griff said. "Looks like we'll have to hold off until daybreak."

"Which will give that no-account more time to slip away," Jeffers said. He was a burly man of middle years, his revolver worn for a cross-draw.

"I'm not givin' up until he eats dirt," Griff vowed.

"Makes two of us," Fargo said. Reluctantly, he entered the woods and climbed down. It had been a long day and he was tired and stiff. He helped collect firewood, then sat back and relaxed while Jeffers put coffee on and cooked stew. There was plenty of meat; Jeffers cut it from a dead cow.

Fargo figured the cowboys would stay up late talking but they surprised him. Griff insisted they turn in early so they would be refreshed come sunrise.

Grateful for the quiet, Fargo sat and sipped. Off in the forest an owl hooted. Otherwise the valley was deathly still.

Between the two helpings of stew he'd had and the wear and tear on his body, Fargo grew drowsy. He closed his eyes and settled back and was on the verge of drifting off when the Ovaro nickered. He was instantly awake, his hand on his Colt.

The stallion was staring into the woods with its ears pricked and its nostrils flared.

Fargo had learned to trust his mount's senses. Pretending to be asleep, he turned onto his shoulder.

Black shapes filled the darkness, and one of them was moving. Whatever it was, it was low to the ground, and circling them. It seemed to be limping.

Fargo eased out the Colt.

The creature stepped into the firelight. It was Esther, the smaller of the wolf dogs. She was favoring her left rear leg, and made no sound as she crept toward them.

Where there was one, Fargo reasoned, the other must be nearby. His skin crawled at the thought that Goliath might be slinking up on him from behind.

Jeffers picked that moment to cast off his blanket and sit up. He was the closest to Esther but he hadn't seen her. He looked across the fire at Fargo. "Are you awake over there? As tired as I am, I can't get to sleep."

Esther froze, her fierce stare fixed on the cowboy.

"Look out! To your left!" Fargo yelled, and throwing his blanket off, he pushed to his knee.

Jeffers spun in alarm and bleated, "God in heaven!" He tried to draw.

The wolf dog was a blur. Despite her hurt leg she reached Jeffers in two bounds. Her razor teeth closed on his neck with an audible crunch, and Jeffers screamed. With a fierce wrench, she tore his throat open.

Fargo fired. He hit her, too, because she yipped and let go of Jeffers. He aimed at her head but she whirled and bolted and was in the dark before he could shoot again.

Griff and Billy-Bob were sitting up and shaking off sleep. "What the hell is going on?" the foreman roared.

Jeffers had flopped onto the ground and was in the grip of violent convulsions. His hands were over his ravaged throat but he couldn't stem the spray of blood.

"God Almighty!" Billy-Bob bleated, and scrambled to the stricken puncher.

Fargo heaved to his feet. Spots of blood marked the spot where the wolf dog had been standing when he fired. He started into the darkness but stopped. He'd be a fool to rush into her jaws.

Griff had his six-shooter out and dashed over. "Which was it? I didn't see."

"The female."

"Here?" Griff trained his revolver on the woods. "That must mean Rolf and the other one are out there, too."

Fargo wasn't so sure. Why would Rolf send only the one to attack them?

Jeffers had subsided and was gurgling and gasping.

"What do I do?" Billy-Bob asked, his voice breaking. "God in heaven, what do I do?"

"There's nothing you can do," Fargo said. "Get on your feet and get your gun out."

"But—" Billy-Bob stopped.

With a last groan, Jeffers gave up the ghost.

"Show yourself, bastard!" Griff shouted at the darkness. "If you're man enough!"

Fargo glanced at the body. Yet another death because of two men too prideful to seek a common ground in their dispute. What would it have hurt Trask to lose a few beeves if Rolf had been willing to pay for them? What would it have hurt Rolf to let Trask graze his cows if he got a steady supply of beef for his larder? But then, he was a fine one to talk about pride.

Billy-Bob joined them, his six-shooter in hand. "Do you think it will try for one of us?"

"We'll find out soon enough," Fargo said.

It didn't. They waited for hours and the night stayed quiet. By two in the morning Fargo's eyelids were heavy and Billy-Bob was dozing. Griff offered to sit up for two hours and wake Fargo to take a turn and Fargo took him up on it. He was asleep almost immediately.

It seemed as if not ten minutes had gone by when Griff shook him.

To wake up, Fargo needed three cups of coffee. He was supposed to wake Billy-Bob after two hours but he let the kid sleep.

At the crack of dawn the cowboys were up and raring to take revenge on the killer of their friend. While Fargo stood guard they scooped a shallow grave and buried Jeffers.

Griff said the eulogy, such as it was. "Ashes to ashes, dust to dust. We'll see you in the hereafter, pard."

The blood trail led to the south. Fargo yanked the Henry from the scabbard and gigged the Ovaro.

"The hunt is on," Billy-Bob said.

46

After half a mile the wound had stopped bleeding.

Fargo sought prints but the ground was hard. Often he had to stop and climb down to inspect possible tracks. By noon they had gone only another half a mile.

"This will take forever," Griff complained.

"If you can do better," Fargo replied, "you're welcome to try."

"I'm just sayin'," Griff said. "I can't track half as good as you."

"Me either. I couldn't track an elk in mud," Billy-Bob joked.

On a rise that overlooked a ten-acre bowl of trees they stopped and drank from their canteens. As Fargo was pressing his to his lips a mournful howl rose out of the bowl, pregnant with pain and finality.

"What in the world?" Billy-Bob breathed.

"I've heard dogs do that when they're dyin'," Griff said.

They descended on foot, moving through dense thickets.

Fargo was in the center. He tried to be quiet but it was impossible. They were all making too damn much noise, and the wolf dog would hear them. He pushed through a web of branches, and there she was.

Esther was on her side. She raised her head and bared her teeth and growled.

Fargo snapped the Henry to his shoulder. He was set to shoot when she laid her head back down and breathed in great wheezing puffs. He lowered the rifle and hollered, "Over here!"

Crashing and crackling attended the rush of the two cowboys to his side.

Griff raised his rifle, and like Fargo, lowered it again. "You hit it good last night."

"Why is she just lyin' there?" Billy-Bob said.

"The bullet is takin' its sweet time killin' her," Griff explained.

Fargo edged closer. Her rear leg, he noticed, was badly mashed, probably from the stampede. Since he'd seen no sign of Rolf or the other wolf dog, he reckoned that she must have become separated and was on her own.

"Shouldn't we put her out of her misery?" Billy-Bob asked.

"She killed Jeffers, boy," Griff said. "And she helped spook the cows that killed more of our friends. Let her suffer. Let her suffer from now until doomsday."

"It don't seem right," Billy-Bob said.

"If I had an axe I'd chop off her legs so she'd suffer more."

Fargo shot her in the head. As the blast reverberated off the peaks, he levered another round into the chamber.

"What the hell?" Griff said.

"There's Rolf and the other one," Fargo said, and hurried to their horses. Reining west, he covered several hundred yards before the cowboys caught up.

"Didn't you hear me back there about lettin' that freak suffer?" Griff demanded.

"I heard," Fargo said.

"I don't much like it that you shot her anyway."

"It was the right thing to do," Billy-Bob came to Fargo's defense.

"Do you walk old ladies across the street, too, boy?" Griff mocked him.

"Don't call me that," Billy-Bob said, and changed the subject by asking Fargo, "Why are we headin' west instead of huntin' around for more sign?"

"The only tracks have been hers," Fargo answered. "And yesterday we checked the east side of the valley and didn't find a thing."

"I get it," Billy-Bob said. "You reckon Rolf headed west, away from his shack, to throw us off?"

Fargo nodded.

"He's mighty clever, that mountain man."

"Don't take him lightly," Fargo warned. Igmar Rolf had done all he set out to do, and then some.

"He'll have that other mongrel with him, won't he? The big one you told us about?"

"Odds are," Fargo said.

Griff broke in with, "I hope you two won't mind if I make *him* suffer."

"I never knew you were so spiteful, Wexler," Billy-Bob remarked.

"Why don't you head back to the Bar T and ask Mrs. Trask how she feels about her husband havin' his face blown off?" Griff said testily. "I bet she's *spiteful*. Or ask their kids how they feel about their pa bein' killed? I bet they're *spiteful*. Or ask the other hands how they feel about losin' so many of our own. I'll bet they're *spiteful*."

"I get the point," Billy-Bob said.

Thankfully for Fargo, they stopped bickering. Once he reached the valley floor he cut straight across to the other side and reined north along the edge of the timber. For half an hour he strained his eyes for the slightest sign, and finally his hunch paid off. A set of hoofprints went up into the trees, prints he recognized. "These were made by Rolf's mule."

"We've got him, then," Billy-Bob exclaimed.

"Not by a long shot," Griff said. "This hombre might be old but he's as dangerous as those beasts of his."

Fargo agreed, which was why he rode with one hand always on the Colt and his eyes darting from the ground to the woods and back again.

"How soon do you reckon we'll catch up?" Billy-Bob wanted to know.

"It could be a day or more," Fargo guessed. Rolf had about a twenty-four-hour lead and by now must be forty to fifty miles ahead.

The hours crawled. By twilight they were over the range that framed Hermanos Valley and crossing another. Not once had Fargo seen evidence that Rolf stopped to rest. But then, mules were known for their stamina.

They made camp at the base of a short cliff high on a mountain. The cliff sheltered them from the wind and hid their fire from unfriendly eyes.

For supper Fargo chewed pemmican and drank coffee. The cowboys had jerky.

When the stars blossomed, Fargo climbed a game trail he'd noticed earlier to the top of the cliff.

Far to the west an orange pinpoint danced.

Spurs jangled, and Billy-Bob joined him. "That's Rolf, ain't it?"

"Odds are," Fargo said again.

"Careless of him to make a fire we can see."

"I doubt he thinks anyone is after him."

Billy-Bob grunted. "It must be, what, thirty miles or better?"

"Hard to tell at night, but thereabouts, I'd say." Fargo squatted. "We'll be on our way at first light." Maybe, just maybe, they'd overtake Rolf before nightfall.

"Can I ask you a question?"

"If you have to," Fargo said.

"Is Griff right? He says I'm too soft-hearted for my own good. He says it's likely to get me killed."

"I've known men as hard as iron who went toes up younger than you," Fargo said. "It's not being hard or soft that gets a man killed."

"What does?"

"Being stupid."

47

It was early afternoon before they found the charred circle of Igmar Rolf's fire. Rolf was long gone. They let their horses rest a bit and were on their way again.

The country had changed. It was less mountainous but still rugged.

They were nearer the haunts of the formidable Apache, and Fargo was on the lookout for sign of them.

Griff and Billy-Bob didn't talk much all day. Billy-Bob was in a sulk over how the foreman had treated him, and Griff was in a killing mood.

The sun described its westward arc and was an hour shy of setting when Fargo drew rein in surprise. Not a mile ahead gray tendrils curled into the sky.

"A campfire, by God," Billy-Bob declared. "Do you reckon it's him?"

"Why would have he have stopped so soon?" Griff wondered.

"He reckons he's gotten clean away," Fargo speculated, "and he's resting up."

"We should be so lucky," Billy-Bob said.

Griff palmed his six-shooter. "Let's go find out."

The smoke came from a cluster of low hills. Fargo climbed to near the top of the first, dismounted, and crawled to the crest to peer over. Another hill stood between them and their quarry, if it was, in fact, Igmar Rolf and not Apaches or someone else.

"We should go the rest of the way on foot," Griff said. "He's less likely to spot us."

"Not with Goliath around," Fargo said.

"I don't savvy."

"Our horses can outrun it. We can't."

"You're afraid of a dog?" Griff scoffed.

"Part dog, part wolf," Fargo corrected him, "and it's the wolf part we have to worry about."

"I know I'm worried," Billy-Bob said.

"All it took was one shot to kill the other one," Griff said to Fargo. "Quit scarin' the kid."

"I ain't no kid and I ain't no boy," Billy-Bob objected. "I am as much a growed man as you."

"I'm twice your years and twice your size."

They might have gone on arguing if Fargo hadn't descended to the Ovaro and stepped into the stirrups. He wound around to a narrow flat and across to the next hill. From there on he was careful not to make any more noise than he could help. He climbed halfway, slid down, shucked the Henry, and cat-footed to the crown.

Below, a stand of oaks and cottonwoods covered half an acre. The smoke came from the thickest part of the growth.

"We can't see who it is," Billy-Bob whispered.

"Stay here," Fargo said, and started down on his belly.

"Like hell," Griff declared, sliding after him.

"You're not leavin' me here," Billy-Bob said, and dropped to his stomach, too.

Fargo had a reason for wanting to do it alone; one man stood less chance of being spotted. He continued to the bottom and crouched behind an oak. He looked through the trees but still couldn't see the fire.

Motioning for the cowboys to stay there, Fargo glided toward the smoke. But once again the pair did as they pleased and slunk in his footsteps.

Ahead, red and orange flickered.

Fargo spied the mule, tied to a tree. There was no sign of Rolf, though, and that bothered him. Where could the man have gotten to? he wondered.

The answer came in a snarl behind him.

Fargo spun and saw Goliath leap on Billy-Bob and bear him to the ground. Billy-Bob yelped in fear and Griff's six-gun banged.

About to shoot, Fargo was slammed into from behind. The forced knocked the Colt from his hand and sent him to his hands and knees.

"You couldn't leave well enough alone," Igmar Rolf said in his ear.

Fargo drove his head back. The crunch of Rolf's nose was simultaneous with another cry from Billy-Bob. But there was nothing Fargo could do for the young cowboy. He had his own dilemma. His head was struck a glancing blow and he rolled onto his back, dazed.

Rolf sneered down at him. "Now I finish you," he said, and raised the Hawken to hit him again.

Fargo kicked Rolf in the knee. The mountain man bellowed and nearly buckled, and staggered back.

Glancing right and left, Fargo saw the Colt. He lunged and grabbed it and was turning to shoot Rolf when a shriek snapped him toward the cowboys. Billy-Bob was on his back, clutching his right arm, which was torn open from the wrist to the elbow. The young puncher was gaping in shock at Griff Wexler, whose throat was clamped in Goliath's maw. The giant beast was on its hind legs, its forepaws on Griff's shoulders, and it was shaking the foreman as dog might shake a stick.

Instinct made Fargo whirl.

Igmar Rolf was taking aim with the Hawken.

Fargo fired as Rolf fired, fired as Rolf rocked onto his heels, fired as Rolf's eyes rolled up into his head.

"Skye! Look out!" Billy-Bob screamed.

Fargo pivoted on a heel. Goliath had let go of Griff and was almost on him. He fired a split second before the brute slammed into him. He went down hard, the wolf dog's blood-flecked teeth straining for his throat, his left arm all that kept it at bay. He had one shot left in the Colt and he jammed it against Goliath's throat, thumbed back the hammer, and squeezed. Hair and blood burst from the wolf dog's neck but it had no more effect than if Fargo had pinched him except that Goliath snarled and strained harder to reach his jugular.

Fargo pounded the Colt against Goliath's head. It, too, had no effect. He smashed it against an eye. Goliath's fangs were so close that Fargo could feel the beast's hot breath on his skin. He tried to hike his leg so he could get at the Arkansas toothpick in his boot but his leg was pinned.

Fargo sensed that in another moment Goliath would rip

into him. Goliath seemed to sense it, too. Fargo would swear the wolf dog's mouth spread in a grin. And then a pistol muzzle was shoved into Goliath's ear and there was the boom of a shot.

Goliath's great body sagged.

Fargo lay gasping for breath, eye to eye with the four-legged devil that had almost killed him. Anger welled, and he shoved the heavy body off.

"I did good, didn't I, pard?" Billy-Bob said, swaying. In his right hand was his smoking revolver. His left arm dripped red drops.

"You did damn good," Fargo said, sitting up. He pushed to his feet just as the young cowboy's knees gave out. Catching, him, Fargo lowered him to the ground.

"I'm awful woozy," Billy-Bob said.

"You've lost a lot of blood."

"Am I goin' to die?"

"Not if I can help it."

Fargo fetched his canteen, used the toothpick to cut the sleeve away from the arm, and cleaned the bite marks. There were three, one a lot deeper than the others. He had a needle and thread he seldom used but he used them now to stitch the bites.

Billy-Bob grit his teeth and winced but didn't cry out.

A dead squirrel, partially skinned, lay near the fire. Apparently they had interrupted Rolf in the act of preparing a meal. Fargo finished the skinning, helped himself to a pot from the mule, along with flour, and soon had stew simmering.

"Poor Griff," Billy-Bob said, sadly gazing at the foreman. "He tried to pull it off me."

"Hush and rest," Fargo directed. "I'll see to the body."

"You fixin' to bury Rolf and that pet of his, too?"

"Hell, no," Fargo said. "I'll drag them off and leave them to rot."

"You're a hard gent, mister," Billy-Bob said, grinning.

"Hard enough."

After they ate Billy-Bob slipped into a deep sleep. Fargo did as he said he was going to, and when he came back, the young puncher was still slumbering.

The moon rose, with its celestial court of stars. As tired as

Fargo was, he couldn't get to sleep. Well past midnight his body gave in but his rest wasn't peaceful. Any noise woke him.

Billy-Bob was all set to light a shuck the next morning but Fargo wanted him to stay put and rest.

"I don't much like bein' babied."

"How do you feel about being dead?" Fargo rejoined. "Another day won't hurt to be sure you're all right."

Reluctantly, Billy-Bob accepted the need to rest.

The next morning dawned bright and clear. They were up early. Billy-Bob flexed and stretched and hopped up and down a few times.

"Good as new," he crowed. "We can head back now."

They climbed on their horses and Fargo reined the Ovaro close to Billy-Bob's mount and held out his hand.

"What's this?" Billy-Bob said, shaking.

"This is where we part company. Can you find your way back on your own?"

"Easy as pie," Billy-Bob said. "But why ain't you comin'? What about that pretty sheepherder gal who was makin' eyes at you? A feller could get lost in eyes like hers."

"I'm a scout," Fargo said. "It's my job not to get lost."

He touched his brim and reined to the south and didn't look back.

LOOKING FORWARD!
The following is the opening section of the next novel in the exciting *Trailsman* series from Signet:

TRAILSMAN #363
DEATH DEVIL

The Ozark Mountains, 1861—where hate ran rampant and life was cheap.

Skye Fargo was deep in the Ozark Mountains. He was riding along a dirt road enjoying the warmth of the sun on his face and the light breeze that stirred the oaks and spruce when out of nowhere trouble kicked him in the teeth.

A big man, wide of shoulder and slim at the hips, Fargo wore buckskins. They were stock in trade for scouts, and Fargo was one of the best. Around his throat was a red bandanna, in a holster on his hip a Colt. The stock of a Henry poked from the saddle scabbard.

The Ovaro under him was often called a pinto by those who couldn't tell the difference. A splendid stallion, Fargo had ridden it for years.

Hoofprints pockmarked the dust of the road. The ruts of wagons ran deeper.

Fargo was cutting through the mountains to reach Fort McHenry. He was to report for a scouting job.

There were no Indians in the Ozarks; they had been pushed out by whites. Outlaws were few and far between. For once Fargo could relax.

That changed when the big man came to a junction and drew rein. He was sitting there watching a pair of red-tailed hawks pinwheel high in the vault of blue when the pounding of hooves and the clatter of wagon wheels drew his gaze to the south.

A black buggy came thundering around a bend, a stanhope with a closed back, the horse galloping hell-bent for leather. A woman was in the seat, staring blankly ahead, the reins slack in her hands.

Fargo caught only a glimpse of her. To him she appeared to be in shock. He reckoned the horse was a runaway and she couldn't control it. So no sooner did the buggy whip past than he reined in pursuit and used his spurs.

The Ovaro was well rested, and swift. Fargo would have caught up to the buggy quickly if not for the road's twists and bends. A straight stretch opened, and he swept past the buggy and came alongside the horse pulling it. The sorrel was lathered and straining and almost seemed to welcome the reins being grabbed and being made to come to a stop.

As soon as the buggy was still, Fargo reined around and politely asked, "Are you all right, ma'am?"

Right away two things struck him. First, the woman was uncommonly gorgeous. Her eyes were as green as grass, her lips a ruby red. She had lustrous brown hair that fell in a mane past her shoulders. Her calico dress swelled at the bosom and along her thighs.

The second thing that struck him was that she was mad as a riled hornet.

"What in God's name did you think you are doing?" she snapped.

"Saving you," Fargo said, and gave her his best smile. It had no effect.

"From what, you simpleton?"

"Hey now," Fargo said. "It looked like your horse had run away on you and—" She didn't let him get any further.

"For your information, I am perfectly fine. And Julius Caesar was doing what he's supposed to do."

"Good God," Fargo said. "Who names their horse that?"

"I have no time for this. I have no time for you. Out of my way. Your pinto is in front of my wheel."

"He's not a pinto . . ." Fargo began, and again she cut him off.

"You are a lunkhead. A handsome lunkhead, I'll grant you, but a lunkhead nonetheless. Now out of my way."

And with that she flicked her whip at the Ovaro. Fargo had no chance to deflect it or rein aside. By sheer happenstance, the snapper at the end of the whip caught the stallion dangerously near the eye, and the Ovaro did what most any horse would do under similar circumstances—startled and in pain, it reared and whinnied. In rearing, the Ovaro slammed against the sorrel, and the sorrel, too, did what most any horse would do—it nickered and bolted.

The woman cried out and tried to grab the reins but they slipped over the seat and out of her grasp.

"Son of a bitch," Fargo blurted, tucking into the saddle to keep from sliding off. The Ovaro came down on all fours and he bent and patted its neck to calm it, saying, "Easy, boy. Everything's all right."

The buggy raced around the last bend with the woman hollering, "Stop, Julius! Stop!"

Fargo had half a mind to ride on. It was her fault her horse had run off. Instead he reined after her and once again resorted to his spurs. The buggy had a good lead and the sorrel was flying. He'd catch sight of it only to have it disappear around another turn. Once he spied the woman looking back at him. She appeared to be even madder, which in itself was remarkable. Most women would be terrified. A lot of men, too.

Another bend, and the sorrel went into it much too fast.

The wheels on the right side rose a foot and a half off the ground. For several harrowing seconds Fargo thought the buggy was going to go over but the wheels crashed down again. The buggy commenced to sway wildly, the rear slewing back and forth. He heard the woman bawl for Julius to stop. He got the impression that the sorrel was, in fact, slowing, when the tail end of the buggy whipped more violently than ever and it went over.

The woman screamed.

Oblivious, the sorrel galloped another forty feet, dragging the buggy after it, until Fargo again came alongside and brought the animal to a standstill. Reining around, he vaulted off the stallion. He was worried he'd find the woman with her neck broken or her ribs staved in but she was alive and well and clinging for dear life.

"Here," Fargo said, offering his hand. "Are you all right, ma'am?"

The woman looked around in bewilderment and then at him and her daze was replaced by anger. Letting go, she heaved out of the buggy, pushing his hand away as she stood. "No thanks to you, you dumb bastard," she fumed. "You nearly got me killed."

"You're the one who hit my horse," Fargo reminded her. "That was a damn stupid thing to do."

"So now this is my fault?" she said, gesturing at the buggy.

"If the petticoat fits," Fargo said.

She smoothed her dress and snapped, "I don't think I care for you very much, Mr. —?"

Fargo told her his name, along with, "And I don't give a damn what you think." He stepped to the buggy. "But I'll do what I can to get you on your way, Miss . . . ?"

"It's doctor to you," she said resentfully. "Dr. Belinda Jackson."

"You're a sawbones?" Fargo could count the number of times he'd run into a lady sawbones on one hand and have four fingers left over.

"Why not? Because I'm a woman I'm not fit to be one?"

"I never said any such thing," Fargo replied.

"But I bet you were thinking it," Belinda said. "All you men are alike. You think only men can be physicians. My own father tried to talk me out of going to medical school. And the instructors, all men, treated me as if I had enrolled on a lark and wasn't to be taken seriously. Now here I am, with my own practice, and I'm being treated the same way by the very people I took the Hippocratic oath to treat." She had grown red in the face during her tirade. "It's not fair, I tell you."

"Life has a way of doing that," Fargo said as he slowly moved around the buggy, inspecting it for damage.

"Well, aren't you the buckskin philosopher," Belinda said. "Any other insights you care to share?"

"Only that you're not going anywhere," Fargo said, and pointed at the wheel the buggy lay on. Several of the spokes were shattered. "I was going to find a pole and see about getting you on your way, but without a wheel there's not much point."

"Oh no." Belinda came over and sank to her knees. "Can't we fix it somehow?"

"I don't usually carry spokes in my saddlebags," Fargo remarked.

"A philosopher and a humorist," Belinda said. "Do you cook as well?"

"Lady," Fargo said, "I'm a scout."

"I was only joking." Belinda and moved around to the other side and groped under the seat. "I guess you'll have to take me. I can't afford more delays."

"Take you where?"

"To the McWhertle farm. Their youngest girl is sick. They sent word over an hour ago. I was on my way there when you spooked my horse."

"I'm not the one with the whip," Fargo said.

"There you go again." Belinda stopped groping and pulled a black bag out. "Ah. Here it is. We'll have to ride double and I expect you to behave yourself."

"I haven't said I'll take you."

Belinda walked up to him. Most of the color had faded from her face but her eyes were flashing. "Listen to me. Their girl is ten years old. From what they told me it sounds serious. I have to reach her as quickly as possible."

"That's why you were driving your buggy so fast," Fargo realized.

Belinda moved to the Ovaro and held her arms aloft. "Are you going to be a gentleman or must I climb on by myself?"

"What about your horse?" Fargo proposed. "I'll strip off the harness and you can ride it."

"Bareback?" Belinda waggled her arms. "I don't ride well, I'm afraid. If I could, do you think I'd be using a buggy? No, we'll leave it here and I'll retrieve it on my way back to Ketchum Falls."

"That a town?" Fargo asked. If it was, he'd never heard of it.

"A settlement, more like." Belinda waggled her arms some more. "Do I have to light a fire under you? If you were any slower you'd be a turtle. Time's a-wasting."

Fargo sighed. He set the black bag down, swung her up, and gave the bag to her. Carefully forking leather so as not to bump her with his leg, he suggested, "Wrap your arm around my waist so you don't fall off."

"Your shoulder will do nicely."

"Suit yourself." Fargo clucked to the Ovaro and felt her fingers dig deeper. "Keep on north, I take it?"

"For a couple of miles yet, yes. We'll come to an orchard and there will be a lane on the right."

Fargo figured she wouldn't say much, as mad as she was. She surprised him.

"I suppose I should apologize for treating you so poorly. But I'm worried about Abigail. That's the McWhertle girl's name. She's a pretty little thing."

"You're a pretty thing, yourself."

"Why, Mr. Fargo. Was that a suggestive remark?"

"If suggestive means I think you'd look nice naked, then yes," Fargo said.

For the first time since he'd met her, Dr. Belinda Jackson laughed. "My word. You don't beat around the bush, do you?"

Fargo thought of the junction of her thighs, and grinned to himself. "I like to get right to things."

"Is that so?"

Before Fargo could answer, a man came out of the woods at the side of the road. The man was wearing a bandanna over the lower half of his face and holding a rifle that he trained on Fargo's chest.

"That's far enough!" he commanded. "I'll have your money or I'll have your life."